CRAZY

ALSO BY AMY REED

BEAUTIFUL

CLEAN

CRAZY

Amy Reed

SIMON PULSE

NEW YORK LONDON TORONTO SYDNEY NEW DELHI

SIMON PULSE
An imprint of Simon & Schuster Children's Publishing Division
1230 Avenue of the Americas, New York, NY 10020
First Simon Pulse hardcover edition June 2012
Copyright © 2012 by Amy Reed
All rights reserved, including the right of reproduction
in whole or in part in any form.
SIMON PULSE and colophon are registered trademarks
of Simon & Schuster, Inc.
For information about special discounts for bulk purchases, please contact
Simon & Schuster Special Sales at 1-866-506-1949
or business@simonandschuster.com.
The Simon & Schuster Speakers Bureau can bring authors to your live event.
For more information or to book an event contact the
Simon & Schuster Speakers Bureau at 1-866-248-3049
or visit our website at www.simonspeakers.com.
Designed by Mike Rosamilia
The text of this book was set in Syntax LT Std and Lucida Typewriter.
Manufactured in the United States of America
2 4 6 8 10 9 7 5 3 1
Library of Congress Cataloging-in-Publication Data
Reed, Amy Lynn.
Crazy / Amy Reed.
p. cm.
Summary: Connor and Izzy, two teens who met at a summer art camp in the
Pacific Northwest where they were counselors, share a series of emails in which
they confide in one another, eventually causing Connor to become worried when he
realizes that Izzy's emotional highs and lows are too extreme.
ISBN 978-1-4442-1347-4 (hardcover)
[1. Interpersonal relations—Fiction. 2. Mental illness—Fiction. 3. Emotional
problems—Fiction. 4. Email—Fiction. 5. Washington (State)—Fiction.] I. Title.
PZ7.R2462Cr 2012
[Fic]—dc23
2011032804
ISBN 978-1-4442-1349-8 (eBook)

For Brian

No pleasure without the taste of ashes.

—*Pablo Picasso*

From: condorboy

To: yikes!izzy

Date: Wednesday, August 31—10:42 AM

Subject: Hello stranger

Dear Isabel,

Sometimes my dog looks like Robert De Niro. She's got a mole on her cheek right about where he does, and she gets this serious look like "Are you talking to me? *Are you talking to me?*" with her forehead all wrinkly and her eyebrows raised and a defiant glint in her eyes. I don't really know what this means, except that I probably spend way too much time with my dog. Her name is Señor Cuddlebones, by the way. Señor for short. I think I told you about her already. And I'm pretty sure it was boring then, too.

Speaking of boring, that has been the definition of my sad little life since I got home. What about you? I'm sure you probably have all kinds of exciting things to do, living in the big city with your boyfriend who's in a band and your fake ID and everything. Me, I'm stuck on this quaint little island, where the most exciting thing happening before school starts is the wooden boat festival, when everybody hangs around the docks and—you guessed it—looks at wooden boats. We do it every year. If I'm lucky, I'll get an organic, free-range, no-sulfite hot dog out of it. This is exactly the kind of small-progressive-town activity my mom loves. She practically had a seizure about the heirloom vegetable seed fair a few days ago.

So what are you doing? It's weird to think about you existing outside of camp. You were this larger-than-life presence for me in those couple of months. It's funny, but I think I spent more time with you than I've ever really spent with anyone. In a row, I mean. Except for maybe my mom when I was a baby. But I'm pretty sure I was sleeping most of that time. And now you're just gone, just like that—poof—out of my life. I know you're only really just a ferry boat ride away, but it seems like a huge distance.

I guess I'm just having a hard time adjusting back to real life. Part of me doesn't want to admit everything has to go back to normal and I have to start school next week. I'm just so bored, you know? It's like I've been hearing this rumor my whole life that there's this big, exciting world out there somewhere, but that's all it is and all it'll ever be—only a rumor. I've never actually seen it. Maybe I caught a glimpse this summer, but now that's gone. All I have are memories, and they're already fading fast. I know I'm being sappy, but that's part of my charm, right? Didn't you say you loved how earnest I am? Sometimes I feel like I'm an old man trapped in a seventeen-year old's body, like I should be wearing a top hat and suspenders and have wrinkles instead of zits, and hobble around with a cane and call Facebook "FaceSpace" or "MyFace." Instead I'm this little stringy mess of nerves and hormones with all these big ideas and no one to tell them to except a fascinating girl I met this summer who exists only via email.

Is it okay that I called you fascinating? My kindergarten teacher once sent a note home complaining that I was too affectionate with the girls in my class. My mom says I'm just open about my emotions, which is apparently a good thing in her world. I did grow rather attached to you over the summer, which I hope you don't find reason to send your man-friend across Puget Sound to kick my ass. He should know I pose absolutely no threat to his masculinity. He'd get here and look at me and be like, "What, this shrimp? Are you kidding?" then get on his skateboard or whatever and fly back to you in Seattle and wrap you in his big, manly, tattooed arms.

I'm not in love with you, if that's what you're thinking. We already went over this. I'm just weird and bored and trapped on this little island, and I'm dying for some excitement, and you're the most exciting thing that's happened to me in a long time.

Love,
Connor

From: yikes!izzy

To: condorboy

Date: Thursday, September 1–4:38 PM

Subject: Re: Hello stranger

Dear Connor, you adorable little freak,

Yes, yes, I miss you too, blah blah blah. You are so funny. Why do you have to be so serious? Do you expect Trevor to challenge you to a duel or something? Do you think he's threatened by my having male friends? What kind of world do you live in? I thought you said Bainbridge Island was a "nuclear-free zone topped with eco-friendly buildings and a bunch of Crocs-wearing, overeducated liberals." That's a direct quote, by the way. Did I mention I have a photographic memory? Just one more thing to add to the long list of Amazing Things About Isabel. Ha! That, and I'm double-jointed. Wow, huh?

I'm bored too, so don't think your boredom is anything special. I think that's the natural state of teenagers, you know—to be bored and yearning and pissed off at everything. I don't know if it's any better for me, living in the city. I guess there's more to do, but you're lucky because you can walk off into the woods or on the beach and just lose yourself. I'd love to be able to do that, just wander off and get lost and have everything just quiet down for a while. Here, there's always somebody watching, some car honking at you, some man whistling, somebody rushing somewhere and deciding you're in their way. We should trade places for a while. You can be a city kid and I'll go ride horses or catch frogs or whatever it is you do in your free time.

Things have been weird since I got home. My mom's been running around frantic because of some Very Important Client, and my dad's been hiding in the basement watching his sports and eating his Cheese Doodles and drinking his non-diet soda even though my mom finds the time in her busy schedule to remind him how fat he's been getting since he's been unemployed. I'm not quite sure that qualifies as domestic abuse, but I wouldn't be surprised if my dad could benefit from a trip to some kind of halfway house for battered husbands. It's just that everything she does has to be so damn IMPORTANT, like nothing he could ever possibly do could even come close. And me, well I don't even factor into the equation because I'm just a kid and have no monetary value. Maybe I should start stripping or something to make some income—then I'd be worth something in this family. Instead, I'm just a drain on the resources of the all-powerful matriarch, my face nothing but a reminder that they once spent enough time naked in each other's company for their genes to mingle.

Teen angst is so boring, isn't it? I try so hard not to be a cliché, but it's like it's written into my DNA to hate my parents and be totally unsatisfied with everything. I wonder if there's anybody our age who actually likes their life. Maybe those purity-ring girls who are too drunk on Jesus to know any better. Maybe I should be a drug addict and run away from everything like my brother.

Let's run away together, Connor. Just you and me and our unmarketable skills. You can write haikus and do video installations, and I'll make collages and construct life-sized urinals symbolizing the plight of modern teenagers. Trevor might want to come along, though. I hope you don't mind. He's not that bad of a guy, and he's really good in bed.

Ha! I wrote that just for you. I am picturing you flopping around trying to regain your composure. You're such a prude, Connor, and I mean that in the most loving way possible. You'd think with such an "enlightened" mother, you'd be a little less uptight. But I guess that's part of your charm.

What about your girlfriend? You didn't even mention her.

You want to hear something lame? Since I got home, whenever I get pissed off (which is often) I pretend I'm back at camp and it's just after the Craft Shack closes for the day and all the kids and other counselors are in their cabins getting ready for dinner, and it's just you and me and the kitchen staff and other random, kidless employees left to roam the deserted property, and everything's so quiet, and the sun is glistening off the water in just that way, and the San Juan Islands are all green and fuzzy in the distance, and the breeze, and the smell, and everything feels perfect. I close my eyes and pretend I'm there, that my life is as simple as teaching crafts to a bunch of kids all day, that I have all this leftover time to myself and I can just do nothing if I want. The strange thing is, sometimes you're here with me, in my fantasy, being your adorable, serious self and not demanding anything from me. And it makes me calm. I bet you never thought you were that important to me, did you? I bet you're blushing again.

Well, I guess it's time to go now. Trevor's picking me up in half an hour and I need to shave my pubes. Ha! Making you blush, even if it's just over email, will never get old.

Like,

Isabel

From: condorboy

To: yikes!izzy

Date: Friday, September 2—7:12 PM

Subject: Re: Hello stranger

Dear Isabel,

Try to shock me all you want, I'm not going anywhere. For your information, I'm not the prude you think I am. Trust me, I have plenty of dark thoughts late at night, alone in bed with only myself with whom to communicate. So there. Who's blushing now?

Since you asked, Alice and I are still an item, although she's been more distant of late. She says she's "figuring some things out" and I've barely seen her since I got back. I'm trying to think what she could be figuring out and why it involves not talking to me, but I'm at a loss. Her parrot, Gerard, died over the summer, so that might have something to do with it. They grew up together and, honestly, theirs was probably Alice's closest relationship. And what does that make me? Less than a bird? Oh, the plight of the horny, marooned poet.

Since you mentioned the "S word," I must mention that I'm dying, perhaps just figuratively speaking, but if it were possible to expire from sexual frustration, I'd most definitely be a goner. Alice was kind enough to bless me with some oral compassion on my return from camp, but then rescinded her kindness at the last minute, just moments before my—shall I say it?—ultimate Thank-You. I was left there in the back of her mom's Prius, writhing in unreleased tension, and she just dabbed at the sides of her mouth with a Kleenex and informed me that oral strikes her as inherently misogynist because the girl receives nothing in return and is effectively silenced in the process. I said I was more than happy to return the favor, or perhaps find a configuration more conducive to tandem pleasure, but she would have none of it.

Honestly, I don't know what I did wrong. I can't imagine a more attentive and sensitive boyfriend than me. My sensitivity to the feminine condition borders on pathology. So why does it sometimes feel like she considers me a kind of danger to her? Was she traumatized in some past life? Does she see me as nothing more than a stand-in for a former abuser? Or is she just a cold fish? Isabel, help me figure her out. You're my only hope.

Hypothermic from cold showers,
Connor

From: yikes!izzy

To: condorboy

Date: Saturday, September 3–4:47 PM

Subject: Re: Hello stranger

Connor,

What kind of disturbed woman doesn't like oral?! On what planet does a wet tongue lapping at one's girlie parts feel like anything less than God's breath? What is wrong with this Alice of yours? I suggest you trade her in for a newer model. She is defective, my friend.

I don't know how to help you, except to remind you that the most important sexual organ for the woman is in fact the mind. Guys can get turned on by a cantaloupe, but girls need a little more inspiration. At least, this is what I hear. I, on the other hand, seem to be more like a guy in this respect. Not that I get turned on by cantaloupes, but bananas or zucchinis, sure. Ha! I think I must have more testosterone than most girls or something. It's like I'm on edge and anxious and I just need my body to feel something else, something different, and sex is the only thing strong enough that works to relieve it. I guess I could cut myself or something, but I'm already enough of a cliché. I don't want to go down that road.

I told Trevor about it once because, all kidding aside, it kind of worries me, this feeling I get sometimes. I'm full of all this energy, way more than is supposed to fit in one person, you know? And I poured my heart out to Trevor about it and it's like he didn't even hear me. He was just all sexy face and saying how lucky he is to have a girlfriend who wants it so much, hubba, hubba. But I was being serious, and it kind of pissed me off. I know most of the time I'm kidding, so maybe it's hard to tell when I'm not, but it'd be nice if someone took me seriously once in a while. That's what I like about you. As much as I kid you about it, it's nice that you take everything I do so seriously. You're the only one who really does.

Your favorite sex fiend,
Isabel

From: condorboy

To: yikes!izzy

Date: Sunday, September 4—1:33 PM

Subject: Popsicle sticks

Dear Isabel,

Remember that rainstorm when everyone crammed into the Craft Shack during free time because it was too wet to do anything outside? It was just you and me and about sixty soggy, hyperactive kids trying to stab each other with scissors. And I was all trying to hand out construction paper and popsicle sticks and asking everyone to please calm down, but it was like I wasn't even there and they didn't even see me. Then you climbed on top of the table in the middle of the room and started tap dancing and singing about surrealism and Dalí and Magritte, and everybody shut up and sat down. This room full of little kids just watched you, transfixed, like you were telling them the secret to life, like you were revealing something really important. Remember? You said, "I dare you to make me a picture of your dreams," and they all got to work, just like that, like you were the president and just told them their drawings would save the country from certain annihilation. You inspired them, Isabel. They listened to you when nothing else would shut them up. They took you seriously. They actually listened to you lecture about art history, and they were like, nine years old. Apparently they knew something your beloved Trevor hasn't figured out. And, by the way, I know it too.

Your biggest fan,
Connor

From: yikes!izzy

To: condorboy

Date: Sunday, September 4—11:28 PM

Subject: Re: Popsicle sticks

Dear Connor,

I don't know how to react to Nice. It makes me uncomfortable. Remember how I'd always pretend-strangle you this summer every time you complimented my drawings or told me my hair looked nice? Well, I kind of want to punch you in the face right now.

In response, I'd like to point out that it doesn't take a whole lot to impress little kids. I mean, why do you think they're always wandering off with molesters? All I had to do was wave my arms around and try to be more interesting than stabbing a kid with scissors. It's not rocket science.

But thank you, I guess. Is that what I'm supposed to say to a compliment? I wouldn't know, since I receive them so infrequently. Not that I'm fishing right now. I'm not, so don't try any of your little tricks to boost my self-confidence. You have an unfair advantage, being raised by a therapist. You know all these secret ways to get people to tell you things and bare their souls. Me, I learned nothing of substance from my Neanderthal father and Executive mother. But I guess my family's not completely useless—I did learn how to argue from my sister and how to lie from my brother. I should probably send them thank-you cards.

Trevor's band is playing at Chop Suey tonight, so I must be off to make myself beautiful. It's hard work being such a jet-setter. My dear sister, Gennifer-with-a-*G*, the self-proclaimed Queen of the Aging Lesbian Hipsters, always tells me our generation is doing it all wrong, that we're all about manufactured style and lack any real originality or substance, like she's automatically superior because she was old enough to remember the day Kurt Cobain killed himself. So I say, "What, like it's cool to still be driving Mom's old hand-me-down Volvo and shopping at thrift stores when you're almost forty?" Then she's like, "I'm thirty-six!" and I have to remind her that's twice as old as me, and then she stomps away with her shitty nonprofit job and two useless masters degrees to go home and listen to her records and read her comic books and reminisce about the days when being poor and overeducated was cool. Except she's not poor anymore, because her wife, Karen, makes a ton of money and they live in a fancy condo downtown. So now I guess she's just a hypocrite like everyone else I know.

I should try to be nicer, shouldn't I?

Yours in eternal bitchitude,

Isabel

From: condorboy

To: yikes!izzy

Date: Monday, September 5—9:43 PM

Subject: Death and dismemberment

Dear Isabel,

School starts tomorrow and I feel like I should feel something. But I don't. I feel nothing. I am dead inside. Do you want to know why?

BECAUSE ALICE BROKE UP WITH ME!

Do you want to know why she broke up with me?

BECAUSE SHE SAYS SHE'S A FUCKING LESBIAN!

Did you hear me? Do you need me to repeat myself?

MY GIRLFRIEND WAS A FUCKING LESBIAN!!!!!!!!

The whole time I was exhausting myself trying to perform acrobatics with my tongue, she was not only not interested, but DISGUSTED with my whole gender. Every time I clenched my teeth and forced myself to act like a gentleman, trusting that someday it would all be worth it, someday I would be rewarded for being so damn NICE and RESPECTFUL, someday God would shine on me and send a lightning bolt of passion surging through Alice, inspiring her to run toward me while tearing her clothes off, eyes wild and mouth foaming, rabid with her desire for me. I kept hoping that all those cramped, lackluster nights in the back of her mom's car were just working toward the moment she'd finally break through to her hibernating nymphomaniac core and go wild. But it was all a lie. All that patience and frustration and talking and hand-holding was for nothing. Because the whole time I was trying to be the sensitive boyfriend I thought she wanted, the whole time I thought maybe I was someone she could love, the truth of the matter was that I was wasting my time. Do you have any idea how that feels? To realize you've been wasting your love on someone for whom it's mentally and physically and spiritually impossible to love you back?

She said I was her last hope. She had been suspecting she was gay for a long time, but she wanted to try dating me because—and I quote—"If I couldn't like you, I probably couldn't like any guy." Do you know what that really means? It means I'm the closest thing to a girl she could find that still had a penis.

It's official: I'm the Last Chance for Lesbians.

What does this say about me?

Your tattered rag,

Connor

From: yikes!izzy

To: condorboy

Date: Monday, September 5—11:48 PM

Subject: Re: Death and dismemberment

Dear Connor,

The good thing is, you don't really have to take it personally. She didn't reject *you*, she rejected your entire sex, which is something you don't have any control over. And really, if you look at it a different way, you could take this as the best compliment ever. What if this just means you're the very *best* of your gender? Did you ever think of that? Maybe you are such an amazing specimen of a man that if a woman doesn't want to throw herself at you and kiss your feet and have your babies, then no man will do. Because you're the best of the best, the cream of the crop, the greatest penis-endowed human this world has ever seen. Alice was putting a lot of confidence in you if she thought there was even a chance you could sway what she knew deep down in her woman-loving loins. Really, you should be proud of yourself.

I'm sorry if I can't spend more time stroking your wounded ego, but I'm a little preoccupied at the moment. You should know by now that I am a very selfish friend, which probably explains why I don't have many. I blame it on the influence of my mother and her type-A personality. I keep trying to focus on you, but my own desires and obsessions keep crowding you out with flashing lights saying "Pay attention to me!" and I have no choice but to obey. I hope you're not offended.

What I'm thinking about is how tomorrow morning I, too, am going to wake up to the first day of senior year. I'm going to put on my clothes and get in my car and drive to that big old yellow mansion full of the rich and smart and superficially interesting. I've told you about my school, right? We're the black sheep of the private schools in Seattle, the indie-rock to their pop music. They're the machines pumping out the future robots of Harvard, Princeton, and Yale while we're the little organic garden sprouting the brains of Reed, Oberlin, and Sarah Lawrence. I know you love it when I complain, but to be honest, I really like my school. The kids in it aren't much to write home about, but at least they're pretending to be authentic, which is more than I can say for the rest of the clueless assholes in our age bracket (present company excluded, of course).

We're located in the heart of the Capitol Hill district, down the street from a women's sex-toy shop and a Wiccan "magick" supply store. A couple blocks away is the community college and a few blocks beyond that is the art school, and everywhere in between are coffee shops and gay bars and ethnic restaurants and beautiful people with big sunglasses and small dogs and reusable canvas shopping bags, and everywhere you turn are these pretty brick apartment buildings full of the twenty-something hipsters that make this little ecosystem so vibrant. It's quite impressive, really, and I'd like to think I'm a part of it even though of course I'm only eighteen and technically not allowed to be cool yet, but I have my sister's old ID that usually works (I'm thirty-six!), and of course I have Trevor when he's in town.

So you'd think I'd be excited about starting school, but I'm not. I'm only telling you this because, well, you're *you*, and for some reason I always feel this compulsion to tell you things.

The truth is, I don't really have any friends, and that's a pretty sucky thing in a school where your whole class is only thirty-four people and everyone refers to each other as their "educational family." I know this must come as a huge surprise, and you're probably catatonic from the shock because you know me as such a charming and likeable person, but if you must know, I have a little bit of a problem getting close to people. It's not like I'm a total pariah. I mean, I'm friendly enough with people and they're civil with me. But while they're all planning their weekend activities and eating the school's homemade vegetarian lunch in the cozy cafeteria together, I'm wandering around Broadway Avenue or sitting in coffee shops by myself and reading. It's like everyone's part of this big happy family, and I'm the weird foster kid that everyone is very polite to, but the truth is no one really considers me a part of the family.

I'm pretty lonely, Connor. Trevor's in Portland and only comes to town a couple times a month. My sister hardly ever stops by anymore, and who knows where my brother is, and don't even get me started on my parents. The only one I really have is you, and you only live inside this computer and in my Craft Shack memories.

Shit, where did that come from? This little bout of pre-school depression is making me sappy.

I'm sorry about Alice. I really am. You deserve someone as amazing as you are, and I know you will find her. Some girl is going to love you like crazy.

Yours in lonely solidarity,

Isabel

From: condorboy

To: yikes!izzy

Date: Tuesday, September 6—9:12 PM

Subject: Please?

Isabel,

Can I call you? I really want to talk to you. It's so annoying having to write things out, then wait for a response, and you never even respond to my questions anyway. Why can't I call you?

Connor

From: yikes!izzy

To: condorboy

Date: Wednesday, September 7–10:13 PM

Subject: No

My dearest Connor,

   We already went over this. I do not talk on the phone. I hate talking on the phone. You said you liked my quirkiness, so just think of this as another one of my wonderful, likeable qualities. Phones are only good for ordering pizza and telling someone you're running late. I assume you won't be calling for either of those reasons, so no, you cannot call me. End of story. Don't take it personally. I don't even pick up the phone for my sister, and I've liked her way longer than I've liked you. Whatever you want to say to me can be said right here. The end.

Isabel

(PS: Phones also give you brain cancer.)

From: condorboy

To: yikes!izzy

Date: Friday, September 9—8:39 PM

Subject: Question

Isabel,

You have too many rules. And you wonder why people don't want to get close to you. Are you this difficult on purpose? You're lucky I'm so agreeable.

Okay, here's my question, and it's important and I really need a girl's honest opinion. And don't do your usual thing where you don't even answer it and just start talking about yourself instead. Here goes: Do you think it's unethical to ask someone out just because you're lonely and you know she'll say yes? Does that count as using someone? Would I be an evil, misogynist pig for going out with this someone and not resisting if things happen to move in the physical direction, even if I know there's no way I'll ever be interested in her for anything more than that? My body is telling me there is nothing wrong with this, but there is the unfortunate problem of my pesky conscience getting in the way. I blame my mother for that. I can practically hear her voice every time I fantasize about taking off Emily's clothes. "Are you treating her with respect,

Connor? Are you honoring her mind and her body?"

I don't know the answers to these questions.

Horny and humble,

Connor

(PS: Have you ever thought that maybe sitting in front of your computer all the time will give you face cancer?)

From: yikes!izzy

To: condorboy

Date: Sunday, September 11—12:17 AM

Subject: Re: Question

Dear Connor,

First of all, there is no such thing as face cancer.

Second of all, I've never wondered why people don't want to get close to me. I am perfectly aware of how difficult I am.

Third of all, maybe you *would* be honoring her mind and body by having a purely physical relationship with her. Girls are horny too, you know. Maybe she just wants you for your body too. Did you ever think of that? Maybe not all girls want roses and hand-holding and moonlit walks on the beach where you bare your souls to each other. Maybe this Emily of yours would be perfectly happy with you using her. Maybe she wants to use you, too. Maybe you should ask.

Isabel

From: condorboy

To: yikes!izzy

Date: Sunday, September 11—11:28 AM

Subject: Re: Question

Isabel,

What, like, "Hi, Emily. What are you doing tonight? If you're not busy, can I use you for your body?"

Connor

Connor,

Maybe something like, "Hey, Emily, do you want to hang out sometime?" Then she says yes, then you hang out a little, then you say something like, "I'm attracted to you, Emily. I'm not really interested in a relationship right now, but I'd like to kiss you. Would that be okay?" And she can either say yes or no. That's it. You lay it all out, completely honest, and she gets to choose. Hopefully she'll decide that Friends with Benefits is a sweet deal for both parties. Case closed.

Isabel

From: condorboy

To: yikes!izzy

Date: Sunday, September 11—9:44 PM

Subject: Re: Question

Isabel,

I feel like I need a mustache and leather pants to say something like that. It works on a theoretical level, I suppose. But why do I feel so weird about it? Why do I feel like I'd be taking advantage of her, even if she agreed to it?

Connor

From: yikes!izzy

To: condorboy

Date: Monday, September 12—11:28 PM

Subject: WHORE

Dear Connor,

    My friend, we are talking about the Virgin-Industrial Complex. What is that, you ask? Well, let me tell you. It is the insidious system of oppression that denies girls of their sexuality in an effort to keep them "pure" and virginal. But what is pure, exactly? Are *you* expected to be pure? Are boys expected to save themselves for "the right one"? Is your sexual activity automatically pathologized? If you decide to be sexual, do you only have two identities to choose from—Victim or Slut? Either someone's forcing you to do it or you're an out-of-control nymphomaniac. No decent, wholesome, sane girl would ever *choose* to have sex. Well, who decided that virginity was such a hot commodity, anyway? And who, exactly, are we keeping ourselves "pure" for? God? Jesus? Our future husbands? What if we don't believe in any of those guys? Who then?

You automatically assume that your wanting Emily makes her a victim. Don't you trust her to make her own decisions? Or do you think she's too weak and too vulnerable to fend off your manly advances? That's not giving her much credit, is it? You're infantilizing her, Connor. By trying to "protect" her, you're turning her into a helpless child.

That's my two cents. I say go for it. She doesn't have to be The One for you to justify hanging out with her. Don't you think The One would be pissed if you didn't get any practice before meeting her? I say go forth and learn how to kiss!

Team Captain of Team Connor Getting Laid,
Isabel

From: condorboy

To: yikes!izzy

Date: Tuesday, September 13—7:32 PM

Subject: Re: WHORE

Isabel,

Why do you assume I don't know how to kiss? I've had plenty of practice kissing. For your information, I am actually quite a catch here on Bainbridge Island. Maybe I'm not tall and brooding and covered in tattoos like all your hunky mainland guys, but I'll have you know that I just so happened to have had sex with TWO different girls, thank you very much, although one was, of course, a lesbian, and the time with the other girl was never technically "completed" due to the arrival of a parent's car in the driveway sooner than expected.

I'm skeptical of your theories, but I'm keeping my mind open. I'm going to ask her out, and who knows, maybe I'll discover something fascinating about her that I never even suspected. That's the point of dating, right? To see if there's anything there to keep your interest? Also, I don't think I'm infantilizing Emily (is that even a word?). How is caring how she feels the same as treating her like a child? Sometimes I think you don't really believe the things you say; you just like the sound of yourself having opinions.

Real Team Captain of Team Connor Getting Laid,
Connor

From: condorboy

To: yikes!izzy

Date: Friday, September 16—11:07 PM

Subject: Hey

Hello?

From: condorboy

To: yikes!izzy

Date: Monday, September 19—7:16 PM

Subject: HELLO?!

This is getting annoying.

From: condorboy

To: yikes!izzy

Date: Wednesday, September 21—8:52 PM

Subject:

Isabel,

I have news. But now I'm not so sure you deserve to hear it.

Bitterly yours,

Connor

From: yikes!izzy

To: condorboy

Date: Friday, September 23—11:04 PM

Subject: dust

Dear Connor,

Forgive me for my absence and my silence and for not spending this time congratulating you on your potential sex life, but I'm in one of my lonely moods again. I asked Trevor when he's going to come up to Seattle next, and he accused me of being needy. Is it needy for a girl to want to see her man more than once a month? Is it needy for a girl who lives in Seattle to get sad sometimes that her lover lives in Portland? "Lover" is such a bizarre word, but it's sadly more appropriate than "boyfriend" in this case. Have I told you that Trevor refuses to call me his girlfriend? His definition of whatever we are is simply that we're "hanging out." For nine months, we've been "hanging out." I try not to think about the millions of groupies who are no doubt throwing themselves at him wherever he goes. I try to be evolved and not jealous and all that. But it's hard. It's impossibly hard. Is it too much to ask for some kind of definition?

Remember how at camp there was that unspoken divide between the cabin counselors and everyone else? No one ever talked about it, but everyone knew it was there. We didn't have to wear their stupid preppy-rich-kid uniform and we got to hang out with the people who actually had interesting stuff to say. We were all just a bunch of misfits doing our own thing, with no need for any centralized government. But the counselors took it all so seriously, all their official and unofficial hierarchies, like they brought their titles of "school president" and "debate club captain" with them to the middle of the forest. And we just watched their little soap opera, how they worked so hard to make sure everyone knew their place. Did you ever notice that certain camp songs were only ever led by certain counselors? Like everyone knew those were *their* songs and no one else was allowed to sing them.

But we had more fun than them, I'm sure of it. I don't know how many times I came across a huddle of lower-tier counselor girls crying by the bathrooms after the campers all went to sleep, weeping about how all the boys liked Annie, and how Annie's cabin got all the good time slots at activities. For your information, I have declared war on all Annies of the world. Did you ever talk to her? Her cabin came into the Craft Shack once on your day off, and she talked my ear off for an hour about how her dad wanted her to go to Yale, and her grandma wanted her to go to Stanford, and she wanted to go to Brown, and oh my god, what a fucking tragedy! She certainly wasn't charming, and she wasn't even that pretty, but she felt entitled to have someone listen to her, even if it was just the crazy Craft Shack girl in the fishnets and flannel shirt. She was just one of those girls who grew up with everyone telling her how pretty and perfect she was, so she ended up believing it, so everyone else believed it too. Oh, Annie, how I despise you and your inflated self-esteem!

Anyway, where I was going with this was that I was thinking about camp and how fun it was, and how I'm convinced we had way more fun than any of those boring douchebags. Were they friends with the townies who knew all the cool places to go? No. Did Roger the Repair Man tell them where the secret beach was? No. If he did, those three idiot counselors from Bellevue could have gone there to smoke pot instead of behind the lodge, and then they wouldn't have gotten caught and kicked out. Did Hippie Erin from the farm share her prized blueberries with them? No. Did Townie Dane take them on a midnight hike and show them which slugs make your tongue numb when you lick them? No. Not everyone is worthy of that kind of information.

My theory is that heaven is different for everyone. It's based on your best memories, and you just get to relive them over and over again for eternity. Same with hell, except the opposite. Like, my version of hell would be the time I found my brother OD'ed in his bedroom when I was eleven, then had to spend the next three days in the hospital listening to my parents fight about whose fault it was that he turned out that way. Except in hell, my sister wouldn't be there to hold my hand and tell me it's going to be okay. It would just be me and my parents and all the sad people in the waiting room, and no one would be telling me anything.

But heaven for me would be summer camp. God, I'm so childish. You'd think I'd pick someplace exotic like Venice or a tropical beach in Belize, but I've never been to either of those places, and the truth is I don't have a lot of truly happy memories. Think about it—camp really is perfect. No parents, no homework, they feed us pretty decent food, and we get to make art and hang around kids all day. But only for an hour or so at a time, because just as they start to get annoying their counselor takes them away, and we're left to go hiking and lick slugs or whatever we feel like. We get to breathe the sea and can see all the stars at night and no one is really around to tell us what to do. Do you realize it's never going to be like that again? Never in our lives are we going to be that free. Pretty soon we're going to have to take care of everything ourselves, we'll have to get a crappy job to pay for a crappy apartment, and we'll spend the bulk of our days doing something we hate.

If you wanted to run away and live in the forest, it would not be that hard to convince me to come with you. I got pretty good at the bow and arrow this summer, so I could do all the hunting.

Landlocked,

Isabel

From: condorboy

To: yikes!izzy

Date: Sunday, September 25—5:35 PM

Subject: Re: dust

Dear Isabel,

It surprises me that you believe in heaven. You always struck me as the non-believing type. But I guess I should stop being surprised every time you do something surprising, since that seems to be the norm more than anything else. Like this sudden wave of nostalgia. Do I detect a tone of sentimentality? I will never figure you out.

So, I took your advice. I asked Emily out. I regretted it almost immediately. She started freaking out about how she's had a crush on me since freshman year, and she has the perfect idea of what we should do on our first date, like she's been planning it for the past three years, and I can plan our second date, and then she can plan our third date, and isn't that just the perfect plan?, and I have the sneaking suspicion she's already planned our wedding and named our babies.

I was hoping I was wrong about her, but I don't think I am. At first glance, she seems like someone who might be interesting. But you look a little closer and realize she's concocted her outfit based on what she can find at the Hot Topic in the

Kitsap Mall and what she sees in music videos. And the stuff that comes out of her mouth is like a commercial on that radio station you have programmed in your car but never listen to, the one that calls itself "alternative" but never plays anything but the same ten horrible songs and the occasional Nirvana classic. The entire evening consisted of her saying "Do you like _____? I totally like _____." Then I would give her a blank look and she'd say, "Yeah, you're right, it's totally stupid." I would try to tune her out and just focus on her lips, and then I'd realize I was objectifying her and my mom's voice would come in loud and clear: "Connor, why are you leading this poor girl on?"

Emily took me to this little hidden beach by her house that has a great view of Seattle, and I have to admit it was a pretty awesome spot. Except it was like fifty degrees and drizzling, and she was determined to have a picnic, but the baguette was soggy and the cheese was so hard we almost couldn't cut it. She presented me with a pipe and said, "I have weed," like I should be proud of her or something, but when I told her I don't really like weed, she was like, "Yeah, me neither," but I could tell she was disappointed, like that was supposed to be her ace in the hole, like she was counting on the weed to make the date a success, and because that didn't work, she was out of ideas. And I just couldn't handle that look on her face, the one where you can just tell she's beating herself up inside, so I panicked—I didn't know what to do, and what's the best solution to hanging out with a girl you don't like who likes you and is now feeling bad about herself? Kiss her, of course. What the hell is wrong with me?

And now I feel like a terrible person because even though I don't really like her, even though I would be perfectly happy never talking to her again, I can separate that from the kissing, I can think of her as just lips that I want to keep kissing and a body that I want to keep touching. Why did I ever think I was any better than this? Because my mom thought she raised me to be something better? Well, obviously it didn't work and I'm just an asshole like all the other men in the world.

At least I was sort of honest. After we kissed for a while, she sighed and whispered, "This is nice," and it sort of made me cringe. So I did what you said and told her I'm not really looking for a relationship right now and is that okay with her, and she said, "Sure, fine, whatever you want," but it felt like she was lying, almost like she was begging somehow, like really what she was saying was, "I'll pretend to be okay with whatever you want because I don't think I deserve any better." And even though I knew that was the truth, I kissed her again, and I kept kissing her, and I didn't stop her when she took her shirt off, and I didn't stop her when she started taking my pants off. And even though it was freezing and raining, I let her get on top of me; I looked away when she pulled the condom out of her pocket. It was too easy to close my eyes and pretend she was someone else.

So what's your great advice now, Isabel? What am I supposed to do when I know the girl is lying, when yes really means no? Is it my responsibility to decipher this code where words don't really mean what they're supposed to mean? What do I do now that I've had sex with this girl I don't even like? Is it even possible for me to not hurt her?

I don't believe you, Isabel. Maybe you're right that there are some people who just want something physical, but I don't think you're one of them. You can pretend all you want that you're a tough chick who would use a guy for his body, but I think really you're a closet romantic, and something like this would hurt you really bad. You act like you're invincible, but I know deep down you want someone to hold your hand and buy you flowers and look you in the eye and tell you you're his soul mate. You want someone who will love every piece of you, even the pieces you can't love yourself. You at least want Trevor to call you his girlfriend, right? You said it yourself. Maybe you say all these things because you're trying to convince yourself you're okay with the way things are between you and him. But really you're not. Deep down, you know he's not what you want. Deep down, you know you deserve better. What's making you settle for him? Don't you realize you could probably get any guy you wanted? Don't you realize you've probably left a trail of guys wherever you've gone who are madly in love with you and would give you anything you want?

Connor

From: yikes!izzy

To: condorboy

Date: Thursday, September 29-10:43 PM

Subject: Re: dust

Connor,

Is there anyone in particular you were pretending she was?

Isabel

From: condorboy

To: yikes!izzy

Date: Saturday, October 1—10:51 AM

Subject: Re: dust

Isabel,

What the hell kind of question is that? I barf my heart out all over the place, and that's all you have to say?

Connor

From: yikes!izzy

To: condorboy

Date: Saturday, October 8—3:18 PM

Subject: nightmares

Dear Connor,

I'm sorry. I really am. I'm feeling selfish and broken. Do you think anyone's ever gotten dehydrated from crying? Like cried so hard all the moisture just drains out of them and their cells shrivel up like tiny raisins until all that's left is a leather-covered skeleton in the fetal position, the skull twisted into a tortured expression of the worst pain in the history of the world? What happens when you can't stop crying? What happens if the calm after the storm never comes? What if it's just storm after storm after storm, hurricanes and tornadoes and every other possible kind of weather, with no end? What if everything's ripped out of the ground until there's nothing left, not even tumbleweeds? What then? What do you do with nothing?

I had a dream last night and it's not gone yet. In the corner of my eye, it is still playing out. I look around my room and everything seems different, like someone came in while I was sleeping and moved things around. Not too much, though, just an inch here and there, just enough to make me feel crazy. I've managed to pee and have a little breakfast, I'm sitting up in bed and I'm writing to you, but I'm still not convinced it wasn't real, that this is real. Maybe *this* is the dream and *that's* the awake and you're just a figment of my imagination, something I created to make me feel less alone. You weren't in the dream, Connor. There wasn't even a memory of you.

It's not Seattle. Maybe it's New York, Chicago, or Boston, some cold city that could be any city. I am older. I can feel the wrinkles around my eyes. I can feel years of my life wasted. I am working at some cheap restaurant that could be any cheap restaurant, the kind with mismatched silverware and fading wallpaper, the kind where men in tattered jackets buy cups of coffee and stay all day. There are some regulars who tip pretty well if I lean over and let them look down my shirt when I deliver their food. The restaurant is in a neighborhood like any bad neighborhood, the kind where crazies come in and hassle the customers for change. On the coldest nights, sometimes they just walk in and stand there until we kick them out. There's one guy who comes in sometimes and just starts screaming. He never hurts anybody, just screams and screams until we give him a cup of coffee and guide him out the door. He likes me the best. He calls me Mary.

There are months of this wrapped up into just a fraction of the dream, identical days multiplied in some synapse to communicate time passing, familiarity, routine. There is time wrapped up in a neat bundle with a tag that reads "Before." The After is implied. No introduction is necessary. There is the guy who calls me Mary, but now he has a gun. He is shoving it in my face and his hand is around my neck, and I guess I just break, something inside me breaks, and when the gun goes off I disappear. Just like that—*poof!*—gone. His hand is around something he cannot see; my clothes and apron and a tray full of lunches are suspended in midair. People are screaming but they sound like waves to me, like slow-motion ocean. So I get out of there as quick as I can, running so fast it's like I'm floating, tearing my clothes off and my earrings and my shoes until there's nothing left and I'm just naked and invisible and wandering the streets of some cold city I cannot name.

I have to go somewhere, so I decide to go to him. He is Trevor but he is not Trevor. He is not in a band and living in Portland. This is a different story. He is just some guy I know nothing about. My subconscious doesn't bother writing him a history, doesn't hand me another package wrapped in synapses. But I still go to him, even though I don't know who he is. I still go to him because, in this dream, I have nowhere else to go.

I am in an empty seat on a Greyhound bus, next to an old lady who sleeps the entire ride. At one point she burps in her sleep, pats my invisible arm, and says, "Excuse me, dear," and falls back asleep. I have nothing with me, no clothes, no food, and it is starting to snow. I walk barefoot along the road. I can't see if my feet are turning blue, if my skin is rough with goose bumps, if my nipples are hard like pebbles. The roads are empty. There is no one to see my footprints in the snow. When a car passes, I stand still, the snowflakes falling around me and melting in the shape of a girl in midair. I hold my breath so no one can see the warm air inside me coming out.

People don't walk much in dreams. Is the journey a waste of the subconscious? Is it only the destination that matters? One minute you are in one place, and the next you are somewhere else. There is a seat on a bus, then a snow-covered road, then a chair in his bedroom. Connect-the-dots without the lines. There is me, invisible, waiting. There is his unmade bed and the horny boy's bottle of lotion on the nightstand, the box of Kleenex. There's the bookcase with untouched Nabokov, Joyce, Kafka, the AP English names he drops to impress girls like me. It smells like him, but not like him. There is something sour, something rotting.

Then he is in front of me. It is him, but it is not him. He is older, less beautiful, somehow smaller, more frail. He takes off his jacket and walks toward me. He is looking right at me, into my eyes. I could lean over and kiss him. I could whisper, "I am here." He hangs the jacket on the coatrack. I hold my breath. I wonder if he smells me. He looks a moment more, but only sees the corner behind me.

The sun has set and there's only a fuzzy blue tinge left of daylight. He turns on a lamp and it casts shadows through me. He kicks off his shoes, crawls into bed, and closes his eyes. I listen to him breathe until all the light is gone outside and everything is quiet. I watch him sleep until he's dreaming, until his eyes are darting back and forth under his eyelids.

I turn off the lamp and everything is dark. I pull back the blankets and crawl in with him, pull the blankets over me. He is naked even though he wasn't before. I feel his warm flesh touching the places where mine should be, his arms around me, pulling me closer, his leg over my hips, his face under my chin, breathing my neck in, painting it with his hot, sour breath. I hear him groan, feel him hard against my stomach, his hands grabbing at any part of me they can find.

But I know it is not me he is grabbing for. It is dark and I am invisible. He is asleep, and could be dreaming of anyone. But this has to be enough because it's all I have. So I guide him inside me. His back arches and his hands grab blankets. I am on top of him, his hands on my hips, on my back, pulling me closer, his chest against mine. I can feel his heartbeat fighting mine, his nails digging into my back, his arms squeezing me closer like he wants to consume me, like he wants to destroy me. I would let him. I would let him eat me if he wanted to. I would let him do anything.

I cannot tell if his eyes are open or closed. I cannot see anything, not his face, not his body, not his mouth, open and wanting. I can just feel his hot breath on my neck, his hands around my ribs. I can hear his small, deep moans, my own, our bodies moving between sheets, the headboard's soft thump against the wall. These are the only sounds in the world. We are the only two people. There is nothing to feel except him inside me, his body against the hole where I should be. He is making me exist. His desire is tracing a shadow around me. Everything is touching and connected and glued together, the sweat making oceans across our skin. There is nothing to hear but his voice gasping my name, but it is not my name, it is any name, a blank space, and that is when we both come, when the world stops and turns black and nothing will ever be the same again.

He collapses with a sigh and I am still on top of him. I cannot see him but I can paint his face on the darkness. My fingers move across his closed eyelids, his strong nose, his soft mouth. His breathing slows and he lets out a little whine as his hands move me off of him. He is done with me. He turns to his side and returns to sleep like nothing happened.

I wash up in the dirty bathroom that smells like the worst parts of him. I am not surprised to not see myself in the mirror. I rub some toothpaste on my teeth, drink water from the faucet, feel it pass right through me. I hear an ambulance somewhere in the distance and the dream starts slipping away, and I know then that I'm not just invisible. I'm even less than that. I am nothing.

Connor, can you imagine what it feels like to wake up and realize you're dead? That you love someone who can't even see you? I am tired, Connor. I am so tired I don't want to wake up.

Isabel

Dear Isabel,

You're scaring me. If this is just one of your drama-queen performances where you make me worry for no reason, then I'm really mad at you and expect you to make it up to me with a care package of fresh-baked brownies and naked photos. If you're serious, then I don't really know what to say. Do you expect me to know what to say? Or is everything you ask rhetorical? What kind of conversation do you expect to have if you keep asking questions no one can answer?

It was a dream, Isabel. That's all. You woke up and now it's over. Okay? You don't need to cry anymore. That was fake and this is real and there are bigger problems than you being invisible, like war and famine and racism and homophobia and genocide and my American History paper due on Wednesday.

I'm tired too, Isabel. Everyone is. You're not the only person in the world, invisible or imaginary or dead or whatever else you can dream up. You're not the only one who feels pain. Although of course yours is prettier and more eloquent than most, and your theatrics are far more compelling. I'd love to wrap myself inside your sadness and pretend it is mine. You could sell those tears of yours. What do you say we go into business? I'll be the pimp for your sadness. We'll make a fortune.

Love,
Connor

From: condorboy

To: yikes!izzy

Date: Saturday, October 15—10:32 AM

Subject: Re: nightmares

Dear Isabel,

Are you still sleeping?

Missing you,

Connor

From: condorboy

To: yikes!izzy

Date: Thursday, October 20—8:42 PM

Subject: Re: nightmares

Isabel,

    WAKE UP!

Please,

Connor

From: condorboy

To: yikes!izzy

Date: Tuesday, October 25—4:52 PM

Subject: Re: nightmares

Dear Isabel,

I'm sorry if I offended you. I didn't mean to sound so harsh. I guess we can both be pretty selfish sometimes, both wanting all the attention, and it's usually you who wins. I guess I resent you for that—for winning, for deserving it more than me.

You've read *One Flew Over the Cuckoo's Nest*, right? Remember how the Indian guy was always talking about how big McMurphy was, not physically bigger, but big in a different way? That's like you. You're like my McMurphy. You're wild and loud and you say everything I don't have the guts to. You're the one with the balls, and I'm just the puppy who follows you around, the stuttering kid who needs you to speak for me and make me strong. I can't stand it when you're weak, Isabel. It doesn't feel right.

I want to be big like you, Isabel. I want to be the one to get all the attention. I want someone to think of me the way I think of you.

You weren't serious, were you? About not wanting to wake up? Isabel, you are so much more than your pain.

Please write back.

Your devoted fan,

Connor

From: yikes!izzy

To: condorboy

Date: Sunday, October 30—2:12 AM

Subject: Re: nightmares

Dear Connor,

    I didn't mean to scare you. You were right about everything. I make myself sick. I wanted to write, but I couldn't. Nothing I could say was worth saying to you. It was all more of the same sad, self-indulgent crap spinning itself into knots inside my head. My laptop was sitting next to my bed and I knew you were inside, but I couldn't bring myself to open it.

Not worthy of your devotion,

Isabel

From: condorboy

To: yikes!izzy

Date: Sunday, October 30—11:06 AM

Subject: Re: nightmares

Isabel,

Thank you for getting back to me. I was starting to worry. Are you okay? Is there anything I can do to help?

It's Halloween tomorrow. Do you need me to come over and protect you from ghosts?

Boo,

Connor

From: yikes!izzy

To: condorboy

Date: Saturday, November 5–4:11 PM

Subject: sorry

Connor,

You're sweet. I've never met your dog, but I'm sure she's sweet too. Just one big, sweet happy Connor family. I'm actually feeling better already. Sometimes I just get sad and melodramatic, and then I snap out of it. It must be PMS or the seasons changing or something. I mean it. Don't worry about me.

The ghosts didn't get me. I spent Halloween watching reality television, which was even scarier.

Apologies,

Isabel

From: condorboy

To: yikes!izzy

Date: Sunday, November 6—10:18 AM

Subject: Re: sorry

Dear Isabel,

I'm glad you're feeling better, but even if it's just PMS, it's really fucking bad, not-normal PMS, and maybe you should talk to someone about it. Like a doctor. But of course I can't make you do anything. Especially over email. Maybe if I could TALK TO YOU ON THE PHONE I could talk some sense into you. Why do you have to be so stubborn?

Exasperated,

Connor

From: yikes!izzy

To: condorboy

Date: Tuesday, November 8–10:45 PM

Subject: change of subject

Dear Connor,

 You're so cute when you're paranoid.

 How are things going with Emily?

Isabel

From: condorboy

To: yikes!izzy

Date: Wednesday, November 9—8:11 PM

Subject: Re: change of subject

Dear Isabel,

I think that's the first time you've ever asked me anything specific about my life. I'm touched. For your information, Emily's fine. I think. That's what she says, anyway, but I have learned not to trust anything that comes out of her mouth. I ended up being able to sever the faux romance, but not before a couple more clandestine meetings in the mist. Every time I think of her, I get a mix of shame and horniness. I imagine this is how Catholics must feel most of the time. Every time I tried to broach the subject of our not being compatible, or just wanting to be friends, or whatever excuse I came up with that sounded nicer than "I don't find you particularly interesting and I don't like you all that much," she would get this little glint in her eye and whisper something in my ear that would make me completely forget the whole point of the conversation. It's like she could sense that I was about to break up with her, and she went into stealth self-defense mode, which consisted entirely of distracting me with promises of sex. I am a horrible, weak person for being so easily persuadable.

It finally ended when she started talking about having me over for dinner with her family. I had to draw the line somewhere, and I guess that's where my tolerance for my own evil behavior gave out. The thought of sitting down to eat with people who love her and pretending to feel anything close to that for their one and only daughter—I am just not capable of that. So I said something like, "Emily, remember when I said I wasn't looking for a relationship right now?" and she sort of deflated right there in front of me, and I thought for a second that I should take it all back, that I should pretend to love her if it meant she wouldn't look so broken. But I was able to explain how it didn't feel right for us to keep having sex, and it wasn't fair to her, and I really like her as a friend, and I hope she doesn't hate me, and then she said, "No, I don't hate you. I wish I could, but you're just too nice," and I think I'm supposed to take that as a compliment, but somehow it feels like an insult.

So I drove her home, and we hugged, and she didn't look at me as she said, "See you later," and got out of the car, and as she walked into her house this sad song started playing on the radio and it really started pouring, and it was so much like a movie I wanted to puke.

So I am alone again. To emphasize this fact, Alice came over yesterday with a shopping bag full of stuff I left at her house. Two books, one dirty sock, a sweater, and a handful of condoms I picked up at the teen health center. "I won't be needing these," she said, and I said, "Me neither," and she just rolled her eyes and stormed out the door like it was somehow my fault that she is the only single lesbian on Bainbridge Island below the age of forty.

Lonely,
Connor

From: yikes!izzy

To: condorboy

Date: Sunday, November 13—12:14 AM

Subject: Re: change of subject

Dear Connor,

Why are you wasting your precious time and superior intellect on these silly high school girls? Seriously, they're beneath you. If you don't watch out, your life is going to resemble a cheesy teen romantic comedy with a really bad soundtrack of two-minute songs by poseur-punk one-hit wonders. Please don't let that happen. I don't know if I could talk to you anymore. I know it sounds harsh, but sometimes the truth hurts, Connor.

Concerned,

Isabel

From: condorboy

To: yikes!izzy

Date: Tuesday, November 15—9:27 PM

Subject: turkey

Dear Isabel,

Thank you for your brilliant insight into possible movie options for my life story. I will take your comments into consideration. I'll talk to my agent and get back to you.

I just realized Thanksgiving is next week. Yay. Turkey.

Why won't it stop raining?

Connor

From: yikes!izzy

To: condorboy

Date: Friday, November 25—11:52 PM

Subject: re: turkey

Dear Connor,

Sorry for the lapse in writing. I'm surprised you didn't scold me. Are you losing interest in me? Figures.

Let's see. What can I tell you about turkey? Well, I believe my family has a unique reaction to the tryptophan. Rather than getting peaceful and sleepy like most other humans, it makes us volatile and cranky. Case in point: Thanksgiving dinner. I have to admit, I had my hopes up. I should know better by now, but I can't help the naive hope that someday my family will be functional. It was the first time we were all going to be together in months, my brother actually had a job, and my sister and her girlfriend were going to announce that they're having a baby with top-of-the-line donor sperm—all good news, I assumed. But that would be someone else's family. Mine doesn't know how to do anything besides fight.

I should have known something was off when Mom announced she was going to have the whole thing catered. Her official statement was this: "With the way things are going with the Rochester account, I'm just too busy to cook right now," like anyone even expected her to cook in the first place, and like anyone even knows or cares what the Rochester account is. My dad said he'd cook, and I said I'd help him, like we're doing all the time already, but she wouldn't hear it. Something about "having the kitchen all tied up" bothered her. It didn't make any sense. But I should be used to that by now. When she's stressed out, sometimes she'll just announce these new, weird rules that everyone has to follow all of a sudden. Like one time (I think it was the Billings account), she decided we needed to have a shoeless house, so everyone had to take their shoes off at the front door and wear slippers. That lasted about two weeks. Or another time (I believe it was the James account), three people had caught meningitis in Everett, which the local news declared an outbreak, so Mom wanted us to soak all of our dishes in bleach water after washing. We didn't even attempt to do that one, so she pouted and wouldn't talk to us for two days.

It's like she falls apart and the only thing that'll hold her together is feeling like she's in control of everything around her, so she makes up these imaginary things to be in control of, and we're supposed to be her puppets. Since Dad hasn't been working lately, he has no defense, so he's just like, "Yes, dear," and does whatever she says, then hides in his "office" in the basement to drink his cheap beer when no one's looking. My brother and sister are lucky because they haven't lived here in a long time, but I remember how my sister would try to fight back and my brother would just shut down and hide. We all have our own particular ways of dealing, I guess. Me, I don't think I've really found mine yet. Sometimes I try to do what she wants, but it never seems like enough, like no matter what I do, she's never happy and always stressed out, so then I give up for a while. But then I think she hates me, so I try to make her happy again, but it still doesn't work.

So yeah, Thanksgiving. My sister and her partner, Karen, showed up, and I don't know what came over me, but I kind of started crying as soon as

I saw them. My mom was in the kitchen telling the caterers where to put everything, and Dad was hiding somewhere far away from the kitchen, and then all of a sudden there was my sister and I just sort of lost it. She's been coming around to the house less and less, and even though she meets me a lot after school for coffee and I go over to her condo sometimes, it's just not the same as living with her when she moved back home after college, when I could see her whenever I felt like it. It's just me and my crazy parents in this big, empty house, and she's across town starting a new family, and I just miss her. I really, really miss her. So there I was crying, so she hugged me, and Karen was standing there patting me on the back like an idiot, and it made me so mad, like can't I have one moment alone with my sister, or do you always have to be a fucking "unit" now?

And maybe I had a chance to say something, but just then my mom comes in wearing an apron, like she expects us to fall for her Thanksgiving Mom costume, and she's like "Karen, Gennifer, *darlings*!" and Dad decides to come out of the basement because now that the sane people have arrived he figures he's probably safe from Mom's wrath for a while. So everyone hugs and Dad pours some wine, except Karen says, "None for me, thanks," and she and Gennifer look at each other in this way my parents have probably never looked at each other. And I try to share the look with them because I know what they're smiling about and I want to be included; I keep staring at them, waiting for them to look at me and smile too, but it's like I'm not even there. It's just the two of them and the possible maybe-life inside Karen. *That* is their family. Not me. I'm stuck with the other two people in the room, the ones who are oblivious to everything.

We're all sitting around in the living room, and Mom only checks her watch once and doesn't even complain about Jesse being late, so things are looking pretty good for a while. Gennifer says, "Karen and I have something to tell you," and they give each other that look again. Dad smiles and puts his glass of wine down and says, "What is it, honey?" And I'm thinking, *Wow, we just might have a nice Thanksgiving.* Except Mom has to go and ruin it by saying, "I don't think this is really the best time." Karen just looks stunned, but I can see the black clouds gathering behind Gennifer's eyes. She says, "What did you say?" and Dad picks his glass back up, and Mom starts saying something about how the food is ready and the caterers are waiting on us and could they please try to be a little more thoughtful? And Gennifer's like, "Thoughtful? *Thoughtful? You're* going to tell *me* about thoughtful?" and Karen says, "Calm down, honey. She didn't mean it like that," and Dad says, "Does anyone need a refill?" and the caterer comes in and says the turkey's getting dry. So Mom says it's time for us to all sit down for dinner, but Gennifer says she's not hungry, and just then Jesse comes bursting through the door and says, "What's up?" like he has no idea he's almost an hour late. And he's wearing ripped jeans and a stained sweatshirt, and it looks like he hasn't washed his hair in weeks. The skin around his right eye and the top of his nose is kind of yellowish-brown, like an almost-healed bruise, and Dad says, "Is that a black eye?" Mom says, "Sit down!" and everyone knows she's about to lose it, so we all do what she says and sit down.

Jesse starts pouring himself a glass of wine, and we all look at him, and Dad says, "Are you sure you should be doing that?" Jesse just acts like it's no big deal and says, "I never had a problem with alcohol," and Dad looks to Mom for some kind of support, but she's too busy instructing the caterer where to put everything. Jesse drinks half of his glass in one gulp; Karen is trying to hide the fact that she's crying; and Gennifer is holding Karen's hand so hard it looks like she's going to break it. The caterer and her helper start serving everybody, but the helper stops when she gets to my brother and says, "Jesse?" with a shocked look on her face. He's like, "Oh, hi," and it's totally obvious he doesn't know her name, and she says, "Jane," and he's like, "Yeah, Jane, hi, how's it going?" and she practically throws the food she's carrying at him. Gennifer says, "What the hell was that?" and he says he has no idea but we all know he's lying.

Dad does what he does best and tries to pretend everything's okay, pouring everyone more wine, even my brother. "How's the new job?" he asks Jesse. "Oh, I had to quit that job," Jesse says. "Boss was a fascist." And just then I notice how much he's twitching, like he's grinding his teeth and his leg is bouncing up and down a million times a second. "What?" Mom screams, and Dad says, "I thought you liked that job," and Gennifer says, "Oh, I see how it is. Jesse shows up and everything's about him. Nobody fucking cares that Karen and I are having a fucking baby." Everyone stops what they're doing and looks at her. "What?" Mom screams again, and Dad says, "Oh, honey, that's wonderful," and he gets up and gives them hugs, and Jesse says, "That's fucking awesome, you guys." Karen's still crying, but she's smiling-crying now, and Jesse gets up and hovers over Karen's belly saying, "I'm going to be a fucking uncle," and Gennifer yells, "It's not about *you*, Jesse!" and Karen says, "Calm down, honey," and Mom says, "Everyone sit down!" and Dad pours himself another glass of wine, and I just get up and walk upstairs to my room and nobody even seems to notice.

I close the door and put my headphones on, set the iPod to shuffle, and just keep skipping songs until it comes to something loud and angry. The louder the music is, the less I care that neither my brother nor my sister has come up to see me or say good-bye, and the whole time I was downstairs, no one even so much as looked at me.

Happy Thanksgiving. I imagine yours was splendid. I bet Santa even showed up early.

Love,

Isabel

From: condorboy

To: yikes!izzy

Date: Saturday, November 26—10:24 AM

Subject: re: turkey

Dear Isabel,

Well, I guess you win. I'm sorry your Thanksgiving was so horrible. I'm sorry your family finds so many ways to break your heart. I was going to complain about spending Thanksgiving volunteering with my mom at the food bank in Bremerton, but now I feel like a big, fat asshole. It figures. As soon as I have an unpleasant feeling or a little dissatisfaction about something in my life, I'm immediately reminded that those feelings are off-limits to me. I am not entitled to them. They are there for you, for kids in the foster-care system, and for kids starving in Uganda. Not for me with my perfect little family and my perfect little life on this perfect little island. If I try to claim one of those feelings, it's like I'm stealing from the people who really deserve them. So I just pretend not to feel anything at all, so then I won't feel like so much of an ungrateful prick.

Does that make any sense? I honestly can't tell if it does. Don't get me wrong, it's not like I don't appreciate how lucky I am. Sure, my dad left us a long time ago—but really, who has two parents these days, anyway? I have a mom who loves me and thinks I'm the greatest thing to happen since sliced bread. So why do I feel so weird most of the time? Everyone at school has their little group. Even the people nobody likes seem to tolerate each other enough to sit together at lunch. But I just sort of wander around by myself most of the time. It'd almost be better if I thought no one liked me, if I had some weird tick or social inadequacy that could easily explain my alienation, but it's not that easy. People talk to me at school and invite me to parties, but something's missing on the smaller scale. I don't belong to anybody. I don't have anyone who is *mine*.

Blah, blah.

I'm sorry you had a bad Thanksgiving. You should have joined me and had dinner with a bunch of homeless people. See? How can I possibly complain when my mom's a saint? She's a child psychologist, for Christ's sake. She treats Kitsap County foster kids pro bono. I know I shouldn't be so selfish, but sometimes it seems like her work means more to her than I do. It's like she's so busy taking care of everybody else, she has no time to think about me, let alone herself. Maybe life seems easier that way because she doesn't have to think about what's missing, or the fact that she's been single for over a decade. And I just have to watch her doing this, making everybody's life matter more than her own, and I have all sorts of weird feelings about it. Like in some ways, I'm one of the people she takes care of. But in other ways, I'm always competing with her clients for her attention. All I know how to do is try to keep her from being sad, and sometimes that means trying to be the trophy for all her hard work as a single mom and professional woman, trying to be the perfect and attentive son to affirm her parenting. But sometimes it means just getting out of the way and trying to be invisible, so she doesn't have to be reminded that I have needs too.

But really, how terrible is all that? I almost wish she was a serial killer so I could feel entitled to some goddamned angst like everyone else.

Ungratefully yours,

Connor

From: yikes!izzy

To: condorboy

Date: Monday, November 28—11:02 PM

Subject: re: turkey

Dear Connor,

Let's trade parents. I'm serious. If you're worried about not having enough angst, you can have some of mine. I have way too much for one person.

I'm sad again. I skipped school today and went to the park to read a book I don't even like. Even though it was cold and windy and wet, I just sat there in the grass until I couldn't stand it anymore, until I was shivering so bad I could barely hold my book up.

Maybe you don't have a little dog pack like everyone, but at least people like you. You're the *cool* loner. You're the mysterious guy no one really knows but everyone wants to know. I'm a loner too, but that's because no one can stand me. I don't blame them, really. I can't stand myself most of the time, especially when I feel like this. All I do is lie around and obsess about everything that's wrong with me. My thoughts go around in these little horrible circles, like "No one likes me because I'm annoying, because I talk too much, because I want attention, because no one likes me." I can meditate on that for hours, and that's just one of them. There are about a million others.

Who decided we need to go around in groups all the time, anyway? Maybe it's a weakness to need people like that. Maybe you're just more evolved than everyone else. Because really, isn't everyone alone when you get right down to it? Maybe some of us surround ourselves with people, but the truth is we do most our living inside our own heads, which is a really lonely place.

Love,

Isabel

From: condorboy

To: yikes!izzy

Date: Tuesday, November 29—8:29 PM

Subject: torture

Dear Isabel,

I doubt I'm as evolved as you seem to think I am. And I don't believe you when you say no one likes you. It's just not possible. How could I like you so much? Seriously. You're the most intriguing person I've ever met.

I have an English paper due tomorrow. So, of course, I spent the last twenty-three minutes making this list:

Top 10 Worst Ways to Spend an Hour

10. Writing an English paper
9. In jail
8. Hanging upside down by your toenails
7. Stuck in an elevator with someone with digestion problems
6. At the dentist
5. Watching your mom have sex
4. Watching puppies get run over by tractors

3. Getting buried alive

2. Working at McDonalds

1. Swimming in a full Porta-Potty tank

The good news is you're not stuck doing any of these things.

Love,

Connor

From: yikes!izzy

To: condorboy

Date: Wednesday, November 30—11:53PM

Subject: Re: torture

Dear Connor,

Well, I'm flattered. But I will remind you that "intriguing" is very different than "likeable." I'm sure Hitler and Pol Pot were "intriguing," but they were also murderous sociopaths.

That's a pretty good list. I'd add "listening to your parents fight." And "sitting alone in the lunchroom at school while everyone else is talking and laughing with friends." Unfortunately, I do both of those things quite a lot.

Have I told you about the Two Aris? Well, they're these boys at my school and they're both in my class and they're both named Ari and they're best friends and handsome and perfect and I hate them. They're going to conquer the world. I'm sure of it. One of them was raised in Switzerland and speaks like, five languages and the other one got a perfect score on the SATs. They both have perfect teeth without ever having needed braces.

One of them is dating one of those slutty Disney starlets and the other one got the governor of Washington State to write him a recommendation letter for Harvard. Who does that? How is that even legal? They walk around with their perfect hair that never moves like they already rule the world, and they're only eighteen. Only robots should be allowed to be this confident. It's not natural. The worst part is they're so *nice*, they won't even let you hate them. Today one of them came up to me with this saintly look on his face and asked me how I'm doing. You could practically see his halo. Bastard. Like I'm some charity case. There's something wrong with the world when people like this are allowed to exist.

Grumpily,

Isabel

Dear Isabel,

I'm happy to report that I have made a friend. A real, live boy! His name is Jeremy and he's in my American History class and he wants to be a marine biologist when he grows up. We were made partners for a research project after each of ours simultaneously and abruptly left school—his with mono and mine because her family moved to Utah to join a cult. Of course, I've known him for years because we both grew up here, but I never *knew* knew him, you know? He always seemed to be too much a part of the inner circle, which has never been of too much interest to me.

We make a funny pair because he's pretty and preppy and popular and perpetually perky, and I'm whatever I am that does not start with a *P*. He's also gay, which isn't really the issue—it's that he's spent all of high school surrounded by squealing girls who want him to be some stupid idea of what a gay boy is supposed to be. That has to seriously screw with a guy's head. He's pretty sick of it, which is perhaps why he latched on to me so quickly. And maybe that's why I latched on to him, too, because even though he's always around people, he feels pretty alone most of the time. I knew I liked him after this one time a couple of his followers came by and announced he had to come shopping with them at the Kitsap Mall that weekend to help them pick out dresses, and when they skipped away he looked at me very seriously and said, "I hate shopping. I fucking hate shopping. And what the fuck do I know about dresses?" We've been friends ever since.

All we do is basically make fun of people, and it's nice not being so serious for once. I'm starting to think that the ability to make people laugh is more important than something totally overrated like, for instance, knowing how to perform brain surgery. The government should subsidize the lives of funny people so they don't have to waste their God-given talents doing stupid jobs. When I am president, I'll make sure that happens.

I just realized you haven't mentioned Trevor in a very long time.

Love,
Connor

From: yikes!izzy

To: condorboy

Date: Sunday, December 4—2:32 AM

Subject: Re: good news

Dear Connor,

Trevor's band is on tour on the East Coast, and apparently there's no internet or cell phone reception in that part of the country. Fucker. I'm done with him.

I'm trying to be glad for you that you found a friend, but mostly I'm bitter for still being pretty friendless. The only people I really talk to are my sister and Karen, but I've been getting a vibe lately that they don't want me coming around so much. Karen's starting to show, and it's all they talk about anymore. I'm starting to hate that baby. Just kidding. (I sincerely hope I'm kidding.)

I'm bored, bored, bored. Nothing's happening. Nothing ever happens. There's a pile of college application crap on my desk that's collecting dust. I already sent in my Reed application a couple months ago, but my mom doesn't like my plan of just

applying to one school early decision and seeing
what happens.

Sometimes I feel like I'm barely alive.

Love,

Isabel

Dear Isabel,

Sometimes I wonder if your feelings are really as big as you make them out to be. Like maybe they're just normal, run-of-the-mill feelings but you're better at describing them than the average person. Nobody likes filling out college applications.

Connor

From: yikes!izzy

To: condorboy

Date: Tuesday, December 6—11:12 PM

Subject: Re: good news

Connor,

I assure you, these feelings are as big as they sound. Bigger. Massive. Overwhelming. Monstrous. I'm offended that you'd think otherwise.

Isabel

Isabel,

   I'm sorry I doubted you.

Connor

From: yikes!izzy

To: condorboy

Date: Monday, December 12–11:53 PM

Subject: deep thoughts

Dear Connor,

Today in art class, everybody was talking about Dalí this and Dalí that, like he is the greatest thing that ever happened in the world, like the words "Dalí" and "surrealism" mean the exact same thing. Some genius freshman even thought he and Diego Rivera were the same person. He was like, "Oh yeah, he was that Communist guy who hung out with Trotsky and was married to the lady with the eyebrow," and I was like, No, you racist asshole, there is more than one famous painter with a Spanish name. We were looking at slides of Dalí's most famous paintings, the elephants with the stick legs, the bubble lady, the photo of him with the flowers on the end of his pointy hipster mustache, and of course everyone oohed and aahed at the stupid melting clocks they love so much.

Everyone loves Dalí like he's the only surrealist that ever lived, but that's only because he was a marketing genius and knew how to sell himself. But what about all the others? Ernst, Man Ray, Miro? FUCKING PICASSO, FOR FUCK'S SAKE!!! What about all the *writers* who started Surrealism in the first place? What about the fact that Dalí was kicked out of the movement for being a capitalist pig? What about the fact that Magritte is way more awesome and versatile? Magritte didn't feel the need to shock and show off. He was more classy, more subtle. Like you can look at one of his paintings, and for a second it looks like any old painting. Like that one *The Empire of Light*, where it seems like a totally boring and realistic picture of a house, but then you realize the light's all fucked up and all of a sudden it starts feeling haunted. You start feeling like something's off, like something doesn't add up. And you can't figure out what it is for a while, you just feel it in your gut.

That's what dreams are really like, you know? They're not full of melting clocks or floating roses or people made out of rocks. Most of the time, dreams look just like the normal world. It's your feelings that tell you something's off. Not your mind, not your intellect, not something as obvious as that. The only part of you that really knows what's going on is the part of you that's most a mystery. If that's not Surrealism, I don't know what is.

Oh boy. Deep thoughts with Isabel. That was exhausting. I think I'll go watch some TV.

Love,

Isabel

From: condorboy

To: yikes!izzy

Date: Tuesday, December 13—8:28 PM

Subject: Re: deep thoughts

Dear Isabel,

Still not doing my homework.

Top 10 Things That Are as Awesome as Surrealism

10. Crop circles
9. A grilled-cheese sandwich with tomato soup on a rainy day
8. Lying down in a pile of fresh, warm laundry
7. Licking the slugs that make your tongue go numb
6. Laughing so hard it makes you pee
5. Winning stuff
4. Wikipedia
3. When my dog farts and it scares her so she runs away
2. When little kids talk about imaginary stuff like it's real
1. Total silence

Love,

Connor

From: yikes!izzy

To: condorboy

Date: Tuesday, December 13—10:52 PM

Subject: awesome stuff vs. pretty girls

Connor,

Some things to add to your list of awesomeness:

- The smell of fresh-stretched canvas
- Miranda July. Every single thing she does.
- *Hedwig and the Angry Inch.* The movie and the soundtrack.
- When it's hot and you turn your pillow over and it's nice and cool on your face

In other news, I want to tell you a story about this girl at my school. I've told you about the Two Aris; now meet Erin. She's in eighth grade and she's beautiful. Like really, really beautiful. Like supernaturally, supermodel beautiful. Like if you saw her walking down the street, you'd probably trip over yourself kind of beautiful. Like I know who she is even though she's an eighth grader and I'm a senior kind of beautiful. But she hates herself. It's obvious. She's probably at least 5' 9", but she stoops so low she's practically my height. She's new this year, so she doesn't have any friends, and she's really shy and afraid to talk to people, and she never looks you in the eye. All I can think is that something bad must have happened to her, you know? And it would have had to be pretty horrible if it could trick her into thinking she's so small and not worth looking at.

And of course the boys love her. They're always talking to her and trying to make her smile, and some of them are even kind of sweet about it. But there's this one guy in particular who's braver than the rest, who actually asks her out. And the rest of the guys kick themselves for not trying that, because she actually says yes, and this guy is a real loser. Like carries around a skateboard but can't even skate kind of loser. And he's a junior, which is just creepy. (Yeah, yeah, I can smell what you're thinking. Trevor and me, whatever. I'm eighteen so it's legal now, by the way.)

So they go out, and no one really knows what

happens, but the rumor starts going around that they slept together, and of course she's in eighth grade so everyone's like "Whoa," and Loser Guy of course isn't denying it. But no one asks Erin what happened. No one even talks to her except a couple of guys who think this means it's a good time to ask her out. And you can just see her shrinking into herself. You can see her disappearing until she's barely even there.

Maybe a week of this goes by, and Loser Guy thinks he's real hot shit. Then all of a sudden Erin shows up at school one day and everything's different. Her hair is gone, for one thing. She used to have this gorgeous long, straight, silky hair, but now she's bald. Like completely bald. Not some cute pixie cut, but absolutely no hair. And she's not wearing any makeup or jewelry. She used to dress really cute, like out of a magazine cute, but now she's in bad-fitting jeans and a ratty sweater. But it's more than that. Something has changed in her eyes, like she's not just sad now, she's angry. She's furious. And it's like she's somehow punishing everyone by taking away her beauty. Like we don't deserve it anymore. We abused it and took it for granted, and now this is what we're left with.

What does this have to do with Isabel? you may ask. Well, I'll tell you. It's about beauty and not-beauty, about being wanted and being ignored. It's about how every guy on earth, even the ones who claim to be "evolved," all know to prey on the pretty girl with low self-esteem. It's like an instinct. They don't even think about it. They just see a girl with a nice ass and sad eyes and they know she's the right conquest, the best effort-to-prize ratio. Not too hard to get, and the returns are wonderful. And she probably won't complain when you treat her like shit, which you inevitably will, and she'll keep saying yes even though deep down she wants to say no. Until she can't take it anymore. Until she breaks. Until she finds some way to get revenge, even if it means destroying herself.

Even though I'm loud and obnoxious, the smart guys know I'm really one of these girls on the inside. Trevor knows. He saw through my fake con-fidence and could tell it was just an act, a cover-up for how shitty I really feel. He knows he can fuck his way across the East Coast and I'll still be here waiting for him when he gets back. And maybe I'll try to ask questions, but he'll tell me to shut up, and I will.

I admire Erin. She's in pain and she's miserable and probably even lonelier than me, but at least she did something. She took herself back. Even if it meant destroying part of herself, at least she was the one in control.

Trevor finally texted me last night. He's coming to Seattle in three weeks and wants me to keep him company. And of course I said I will.

Love,

Isabel

From: condorboy

To: yikes!izzy

Date: Wednesday, December 14—5:03 PM

Subject: Re: awesome stuff vs. pretty girls

Isabel,

Why didn't you go talk to her? Erin, I mean. If you can tell she's so lonely and in so much pain, why don't you try to help her?

I thought you said you were done with Trevor.

Connor

From: yikes!izzy

To: condorboy

Date: Wednesday, December 14—10:46 PM

Subject: Re: awesome stuff vs. pretty girls

Connor,

 Yeah, thanks for making me feel even worse than I already do.

Isabel

From: condorboy

To: yikes!izzy

Date: Thursday, December 15—8:33 PM

Subject: pretty girls & kissing boys

Dear Isabel,

That's not what I meant to do. I thought it might help you feel better. My mom's always saying stuff like that—like being of service to other people is sometimes the best way to heal yourself. "The best way to build self-esteem is by doing esteemable acts" is one of her favorite sayings when I'm moping around. I'm not really sure how it's supposed to work, but I tend to trust my mom about these things. If anything, thinking about someone else for a little while means not obsessing about yourself, and that's a good thing, right? Sorry if this is annoying. It's annoying when my mom says it too.

Have you ever tried telling Trevor how you feel? Told him you feel like he's using you? Maybe he doesn't even realize he's doing it. Although, honestly, I find that hard to believe. I hope you're not offended, but he sounds like a real asshole to me. What do you see in him? Have you ever stopped to think about that? You could do much better. Trust me.

I guess you have a point with your "pretty girls with low self-esteem" theory. Guys can be assholes, I'll be the first to agree. But maybe not all of them do it for the same reasons. Maybe some of them aren't predators. Maybe they go for these sad girls because they have some instinct to protect them and take care of them. Although I guess that's still pretty egotistical when you think about it. The guy gets to think of himself as a kind of knight in shining armor, and the girl still probably doesn't feel that great about herself, but now, in addition, she's dependent on some guy. Jesus. My mom jokes sometimes that most of society's problems could be solved if the government provided all citizens with free therapy. I think she's on to something.

In other news, I kissed a boy the other night. It's not as exciting as it sounds, so don't start planning a big coming-out party for me just yet. Jeremy and I were hanging out on this dock Saturday night. Remember how clear and still and weirdly warm it was that night? Somehow Jeremy got a bottle of rum, and I don't even like to drink all that much, but it seemed really important to him that I drink this rum, so I did, and we got sort of drunk. We were looking at the little phosphorescent plankton in the water, and we had a pile of rocks we collected from the beach. We'd throw the rocks in and watch the plankton light up as the rock sank to the bottom, kind of like the sea's version of a shooting star. It was pretty magical, and the rum was making me feel all warm and nostalgic. It felt a lot like camp, except instead of you, it was Jeremy. And I guess that's what I was thinking about when this conversation happened:

Jeremy: "What if I tried to kiss you right now?"

Me: "Huh?"

Jeremy: "If I kissed you, would you kiss me back?"

Me: (thinking for a second) "Yeah, probably."

So then he leans over and kisses me and I drop all the rocks I'm holding and I hear them scatter all over the wooden dock. For a second I'm just in shock, and then my brain registers that my lips are moving and there's a tongue in my mouth, and I'm pretty sure it feels good. So then I relax and I think I'm enjoying it, but then I remember it's Jeremy, and that makes me feel weird, and then I realize I'm just too conscious of the entire thing, and what my brain thinks and what my body feels are just not agreeing. So I stop and Jeremy's looking me in the eye with this expectant look on his face, and I just feel so embarrassed and exposed, like I've been caught in a lie, and I don't know what to do so I just look away and start collecting all the rocks that I dropped. Then this conversation happens:

Jeremy: "So?"

Me: "Hmm."

Jeremy: "*Hmm*, what?"

Me: "Your lips are harder than a girl's."

Jeremy: "What else?"

Me: "I guess it was okay."

Jeremy: "Gee, thanks."

Me: "No, I mean you're a good kisser and everything. I just don't think I'm very gay."

Jeremy: "Oh."

Me: "I'm sorry."

Jeremy: "It's okay. It was worth a try."

Me: "If I was gay, I'd totally be gay for you."

Jeremy: "Thanks."

Me: "Are things going to be weird now?"

Jeremy: "Probably. For a little while. But I'll get over it."

Me: "That's good."

Jeremy: "Someone should start a college that's all gay people, so people like me who grew up on straight-ass islands can be sure to get a date and not get crushes on straight boys all the time."

Me: "Maybe in San Francisco."

Jeremy: "Yeah, I'm already applying to all the schools in San Francisco. Even the Catholic one."

Me: "Especially the Catholic one."

Then we sit there for a few seconds, and it's awkward, and Jeremy says, "This is awkward," and I say, "Yeah," and he says, "Why don't I take you home and we can start forgetting this happened," and I say okay even though I know he probably shouldn't be driving, but I don't know what else to do. We don't say anything the whole way there, and when we drive up to my house, I say, "Bye," and he says, "Bye," and that's the end of that. Everything has stayed pretty much normal at school, except for some little things. Like I've noticed he doesn't look me in the eye as much as before. And he doesn't touch me as much—not that he touched me a lot to begin with, but sometimes he'd slap me on the back, stuff like that. It's like things have turned slightly formal between us. I really hope this doesn't last forever.

I'm confused. I keep wondering if maybe I'm a little bit gay. Maybe my aversion to kissing Jeremy just came from some internalized homophobia I've picked up from the media. Maybe the true feelings were in the moments I was enjoying it. But then every time I think of it, it doesn't turn me on at all. But I have this feeling like I miss Jeremy. Maybe I'm not very gay at all, but I just miss the ease of our friendship. Maybe when you're drunk, kissing anyone feels good.

How are you supposed to know?

Dazed and confused,

Connor

Friday, December 16—11:48 PM

condorboy: hi

yikes!izzy: damn. you caught me

condorboy: yeah, it's like you're almost real

yikes!izzy: almost

condorboy: did you get my email last night?

yikes!izzy: the one about you being gay?

condorboy: . . .

yikes!izzy: what do you think about when you masturbate?

condorboy: WHAT?!!!

yikes!izzy: just go with it. i'm being scientific here. what do you think about when you masturbate?

yikes!izzy: guys or girls?

condorboy: girls

yikes!izzy: always?

condorboy: yes

condorboy: always

yikes!izzy: you're straight. case closed.

condorboy: thanks doctor

yikes!izzy: do you think about anyone in particular?

condorboy: no comment

yikes!izzy: have you ever fantasized about more than one girl at once?

yikes!izzy: like together?

condorboy: jesus, what is this? i'm growing uncomfortable with this line of questioning

yikes!izzy: just answer the question

yikes!izzy: remember, i'm a doctor

condorboy: ok. sure. yeah. what guy hasn't fantasized about that?

yikes!izzy: why do you think that's every straight guy's fantasy?

condorboy: i don't know

condorboy: maybe because girls are pretty and two girls are even prettier. squishy parts bumping up against each other. that sort of thing.

condorboy: can we stop talking about this now?

yikes!izzy: maybe, but then I wouldn't get to rant about why it pisses me off

yikes!izzy: isn't that your favorite thing about me?

condorboy: what?

yikes!izzy: my ranting about things that piss me off. it's pretty much my greatest talent.

condorboy: ok. whatever you say.

yikes!izzy: on that note . . .

yikes!izzy: BYE!

condorboy: bye?

[**yikes!izzy** is offline.]

From: yikes!izzy

To: condorboy

Date: Sunday, December 18—12:05 AM

Subject: kissing girls (continued)

Connor,

I've told you about my school and how every-one considers themselves so "enlightened," right? Well, they're not. They're fakes like everyone else; they just have bigger vocabularies and different bumper stickers on their minivans. The Two Aris are just like all the other prep-school boys in the world. An example: On the first day of school, my art teacher asked everyone who their favorite artists are, and yes, I admit that maybe I was in a darker mood than usual and would have answered differently any other day, but she should have at least pretended to not be horrified when I said Francis Bacon and Joel-Peter Witkin. You should have seen her face, Connor. She probably thought she was looking at a future serial killer. What was I supposed to say? That I love Monet? Edward Hopper? NORMAN FUCKING ROCKWELL?!

Now back to the topic from last night. All the

girls at my school—and every other private school in Seattle, from what I hear—have decided that the new cool thing for the year is for all the girls to pretend to be bisexual, which basically just involves getting drunk at parties and making out with each other in front of their boyfriends. It's not like they have actual relationships. They're just trying on the identity like it's some kind of performance, then they take it off whenever it's convenient. They don't have to deal with the other things that come with it, like homophobic assholes and fucked-up laws.

I was telling my sister and Karen about this one girl in particular who's notorious for drinking too many wine coolers and running around asking all the boys what girl they want her to make out with. Gennifer just rolled her eyes and said, "What a dumbass," but Karen got real quiet and her jaw started grinding, and she looked like she wanted to punch something. Gennifer and I just sort of looked at her, wondering what was the right thing to say, then Karen let out a big sigh and started shaking her head.

"It's not something you can just take off when

the party's over," she said. "It's not something you put on like a costume to entertain your horny boyfriends. Being gay is something people lose their families for. It's something they get beat up for. It's something people still get killed for. It's not a fucking party trick."

Karen grew up in a small farm town in Idaho. She got beat up a lot for looking so butch. Her parents disowned her. She always jokes that she's spent more money on therapy than college and grad school combined. But it's not funny. None of it is funny.

I wish you could meet Gennifer and Karen. Besides you, they're the best things in my life. You should really visit, you know. Soon.

Love,

Isabel

(P.S. I got into Reed.)

From: condorboy

To: yikes!izzy

Date: Monday, December 19—4:53 PM

Subject: Re: kissing girls (continued)

Dear Isabel,

Really? You're inviting me over? Let me think about it. . . . YES! I would love to meet them. I really would. What if I came the weekend of New Year's? I just asked my mom and she said I can even stay the night as long as I don't sleep in the same room as you. As if anything would happen. What a joke. Ha, ha, very funny. . . . It's funny, right?

It's too easy to forget how fucked up the rest of the world is when we live where we do. Mom talks about that a lot, about how we live in a sort of utopian bubble and aren't reminded enough how broken it is outside, how much suffering there is. And then her best friend, Liza, who's always over says something about White Guilt, and then they chuckle and pour a glass of Pinot and go sit outside to watch the sunset. I'm not sure what they find so funny about White Guilt, or even what it means, but I am aware that we pretty much live in a fantasy world. But I'm glad it exists for people like Karen to come to and feel safe finally. But I wonder what it means if the people who were raised here never leave, if we just stay in this bubble for the rest of our lives.

Things are getting better between me and Jeremy. It almost feels back to normal. I think it's because he's started hooking up with this freshman kid he said exuded a gay vibe, so he started talking to him one day, and they hung out a couple times, and his suspicions were indeed confirmed. I asked him if he thought I had a gay vibe, and he said not really. So I asked him why he kissed me if he didn't think I was gay, and he just looked at me like I was a dumb kid and said, "Because you're cute, you dork," like it's totally obvious and I'm an idiot for not knowing about it. But honestly—and I'm not just fishing for compliments or anything—I've never really considered myself attractive. In fact, I've always been pretty insecure about my height and how skinny I am, and my hair always looks like I just woke up, and I have this one perpetual zit on my forehead that never goes away. But I don't know. I guess I'm not the best judge of what makes guys attractive. What do you think? Be honest. I really want to know.

So what do you think about me visiting that weekend? It'll be like the best Christmas present ever.

Love,
Connor

(P.S. Congratulations!)

From: yikes!izzy

To: condorboy

Date: Wednesday, December 21–3:12 AM

Subject: spelling

Dear Connor,

There is something I believe in very deeply. Some people have Jesus. I have English. Here is one more reason I hate phones, specifically cell phones: texting. Sure, it seems convenient, but it is destroying the English language. I refuse to write in text speak. You will never read an LOL or ROTFL or WTF from me. NEVER! Our forepeople didn't work for thousands of years creating this eloquent tool of expression only to have it rolled in the technological mud by a bunch of teenagers who are too lazy to spell correctly. We're getting dumber as a society, Connor, and I refuse to be a part of it.

I'm feeling way better now. Like I've never felt this good in my life. I don't know what happened, but suddenly it sort of feels like sleep is something I've grown out of. Which is fine with me, because I have so much to do. I finished all my college applications in two days. TWO DAYS! I think it's a new world record. And they're good, too. Brilliant, in fact. That's the good news.

The bad news is no one else seems quite as thrilled about my newfound energy. I got sent home from school early today, which was fine with me because of course I didn't actually go home, I just wandered around Broadway talking to people, but I guess my phone was ringing the whole time, but I had it turned off, and my dad was calling because the principal called him and told him I was being disruptive in class because I kept interrupting the teacher. This is what he told me when I got home, and I tried to explain to him that I was just taking an active role in my education by asking questions, like isn't that what education is about? Exchanging ideas? Then he said it was a lecture class, not a discussion class, and I was like, "They are so fucking attached to their stupid definitions," and he was like, "It's not a definition, it's just the way it is," and I was like, "Dad, that doesn't even make any sense," but no one ever said he's the brains in the family. I mean, how much brains does it take to be an out-of-work realtor? Then I said, "How do they expect to be a successful genius factory if they don't allow some sort of discourse?" and he said, "Go to your room," and I said, "Gladly," because really, the only appeal to the rest of the house is the bathroom and the kitchen, and I'm so not hungry, and I can pee out my window if I have to.

Iz

From: condorboy

To: yikes!izzy

Date: Wednesday, December 21—5:01 PM

Subject: Re: spelling

Dear Isabel,

   I'm glad you're feeling better. Did you talk to your parents about me coming to visit?

Love,

Connor

From: yikes!izzy

To: condorboy

Date: Friday, December 23—4:37 AM

Subject: ART!

Holy shit, Connor!

I just made the best art I've ever made in my whole life! Screw those stupid watercolors and wood prints I did this summer. Child's play! Well, to be honest, I didn't actually get to finish, and it doesn't actually exist anymore, but the IDEA was awesome and that's what really counts, right?

So my mom was pissing me off as usual because she was trying to convince me that being a business major is the only way to go, and I was like, "Do you even know who I *am*?" and she started complaining about how a degree in fine arts or creative writing is totally worthless, and then I said, "What about a double-major in fine arts *and* creative writing?" which I thought was pretty funny, but she started screaming about me not taking anything seriously, so I started screaming about her taking everything *too* seriously, and my dad was trying to calm us down, but neither of us ever takes *him* seriously, so she said, "Go to your room," and Dad said, "What about dinner?" and I said, "I don't need dinner," and Mom said, "She doesn't need dinner," all at the same time. So I went up to my room and started kicking things and ripping up all the paper I could find, and that's when I got my brilliant idea.

So I went into my mom's office and found the files where she keeps all the bank statements and stock reports and every stupid piece of paper with dollar signs on it that she saves so lovingly, and I don't think she ever saved a piece of my artwork like that, all the pictures I drew in kindergarten, the little crayon scribbles normal parents proudly display on the fridge or tuck away safely in a cherished box. Some parents have torn-out coloring-book pages; my mom has papers that tell her how much money she's made, and she loves those things like they came from inside of her. So, naturally, I had to take them. I went through the whole room and found all the papers I could find, and I carried the big stack to my room and just started tearing everything up, all of it into little jagged pieces, and I think it took me hours, but when I was done I had a pile of fluffy white paper, and it looked so innocent like that, all torn up, like it never had the power it once did, like it could never have been so cruel. It was this brand-new soft thing, devoid of meaning, nothing but texture.

My mom was in bed, asleep, and my dad was in the den watching TV, so nobody noticed me take the blender from the kitchen. My music was so loud that nobody noticed the sound of the paper and water in the blender being turned into pulp. And the paper was transformed yet again; now it was a big lump of drenched, heavy mush, with this nice, sweet, earthy smell, and I wadded it up into balls and squeezed the water into my trash can; I squeezed with all the strength I could, all the energy that was sizzling inside me, and it made this gray chunky soup that almost looked deli-cious. Then I took the screen off my window and used my stupid Economics textbook to press the balls into the screen, squeezing the rest of the water into my carpet, the 100% wool top-of-the-line carpet my mom is so proud of, and I pressed and pressed until it was as dry as it could be, and

I was just about to start sculpting with it, I was going to make a paper sculpture of my mom, I was going to let it dry and become hard and strong, and then I was going to spray it with a hose so it'd get mushy all over again and fall apart and my mom would be reduced to nothing; all her money would be shapeless, ugly mush.

That was the rest of my plan, anyway, but I never got to do it. Because of course my mom couldn't sleep, because she was thinking about money, so she had to get up and go to her office, and what did she find but empty files and all her papers gone, so of course she freaked out, and of course she barged into my room and found me drenched and covered with pulp, and big puddles on the expensive carpet, and clumps of mush stuck in various places around the room, and she had a sort of meltdown while I just sat there trying to sculpt, and I thought for a second how thoughtful it was for her to come model for the sculpture, but then she tore wet paper out of my hand, grabbed everything she could find that I might want and threw it into the hallway. She was screaming her head off, all sorts of things coming out of her mouth, but the only thing I could really hear was "What the hell is wrong with you?" and that stuck with me for some reason because I was wondering the same thing myself.

So needless to say, I'm in trouble. I'm "grounded," apparently, which is something new they're trying out, and I don't think they quite know how it works because they didn't actually think to mention what I'm grounded *from*. My dad suggested I go to therapy, but that just started a new fight between them about my mom basically saying, "Oh yeah? Who exactly is going to pay for this therapy, huh? Not you, obviously, since you haven't had a job in six months." And then it wasn't about me anymore. I'm not worried because I know they'd never make me go to a therapist. It would require too much work on their part to actually find one and make appointments and so on. So things will probably continue as normal, except they'll probably give me the silent treatment for a while, which is perfectly fine with me.

Iz

Sunday, December 25—3:46 PM

condorboy: caught you again

yikes!izzy: damn you

condorboy: merry xmas

yikes!izzy: bleh

condorboy: what are you doing?

yikes!izzy: bleh

condorboy: got your email

condorboy: so you're grounded?

condorboy: guess i can't come visit next weekend?

yikes!izzy: visit visit visit, that's all you think about

yikes!izzy: do you think you're going to get laid or something?

yikes!izzy: it's kind of pathetic

yikes!izzy: hello?

yikes!izzy: so now you're giving me the silent treatment

yikes!izzy: great

yikes!izzy: fuck you too

condorboy: i'm not giving you the silent treatment

condorboy: i just don't have a response to you being an asshole

yikes!izzy: yeah yeah

yikes!izzy: sorry sorry sorry

yikes!izzy: i apologize profusely

yikes!izzy: didn't mean it

yikes!izzy: been really irritable lately

yikes!izzy: haven't been sleeping well

yikes!izzy: blah blah sorry blah

yikes!izzy: forgive me?

condorboy: i guess

condorboy: so what's your family doing for xmas?

[**yikes!izzy** is offline.]

From: yikes!izzy

To: condorboy

Date: Monday, December 26—8:27 PM

Subject: zoo

My dearest Connor,

I'm like an animal trapped in a cage, pacing back and forth, waiting for someone to feed me. But I just realized they don't have any food! So I'm going out tonight, with or without my parents' permission. My window is not that far from the ground, when you think about it, if you squint your eyes in just the right way. I'm pretty sure I can jump out without breaking anything. Either that or just walk out the front door when no one's looking, which is pretty much always because the front door is in the middle of the house and my parents like to be as far away from each other as possible, which means not in the middle of the house, so I pretty much have a straight shot to freedom if I want it. But jumping out the window sounds a little more fun, doesn't it? Yes. The answer is yes.

Iz

From: condorboy

To: yikes!izzy

Date: Monday, December 26—9:16 PM

Subject: Re: zoo

Isabel,

Do I even need to say "Don't jump out the window?" Should I even bother? I think I like it better when you're depressed.

Connor

From: yikes!izzy

To: condorboy

Date: Tuesday, December 27—11:13 PM

Subject:

Connor,

Fuck.

Fuckfuckfuckfuckfuckfuckfuck.

I fucked up big-time. And I'm not just being dramatic. I don't even want to tell you. You're going to hate me. Please don't hate me.

I cheated on Trevor last night. I know you're not particularly fond of Trevor, but you're the most principled person I know, so even if I was dating Hitler, you'd probably think I was an asshole for cheating on him. I wasn't planning on doing it. I just wanted to go out. So I did. I didn't even have to jump out the window, you'll be happy to know. And I just so happened to park my car a little down the street, so my parents couldn't hear me drive away. But that's not the point. The point is, I drove up to Capitol Hill and went to a bar and ordered a drink even though I hate drinking. And then this guy in an Elmo

T-shirt asked if he could buy me another drink, and I really liked his shirt, and the bartender was sick of talking to me, so I said yes, and then we started talking and I think he bought me another drink, and I clearly remember getting stupider and stupider. It was like I suddenly had this primal instinct to be stupid, and I couldn't stop. I remember asking him to tell me the story behind all his tattoos, and I think I actually pretended to listen to him explain why the copy of Hokusai's *The Great Wave* on his forearm means so much to him, although of course he didn't even know the artist's name, and the girl at the end of the bar had the exact same tattoo and she probably didn't know the artist's name, either, and all of a sudden it seemed like everyone in the entire bar had the exact same tattoos and the jukebox was playing something stupid, and I just needed to feel something and the alcohol wasn't enough, and he was there and he was wearing that Elmo shirt, so I turned to him and looked into his big, brown, stupid bloodshot eyes, and I put my hand on *The Great Wave*, and I screamed over the music, "Let's go to your place!" So we did. And luckily he only lived a couple blocks away because there's no way I should have been driving, but the scary thing is I probably would have, if I had to. My favorite uncle died in a drunk-driving accident, and I promised myself at age eight that I would never, ever, EVER drive drunk. You can't just go back on a promise like that. You just can't.

I know I should feel bad about cheating, but the weird thing is that I don't. I just feel scared. But I'm not even sure about what. Maybe it's scared of getting caught, or Trevor finding out. But I don't think it's that, really. I think I'm scared of not knowing what I'm capable of, scared that I am someone who would sneak out and get drunk and have sex with a guy whose name I don't even remember just because I liked his shirt. I'm scared that I could do even worse. I'm scared of this feeling I have inside like bad electricity, like something burning, and it's making me someone else, someone unpredictable, someone scary. I could care less about cheating on Trevor, but I am terrified of this girl because I don't know what she's going to make me do next.

I feel like if you were here you could calm me down, like your presence alone could get rid of her and bring me back.

Help,

Iz

From: condorboy

To: yikes!izzy

Date: Wednesday, December 28—4:52 PM

Subject: Re:

Dear Isabel,

    I don't know what to say. You say I'm principled, but why do you assume that also means I'm judgmental? I don't judge you for cheating on Trevor, and I definitely don't hate you. I could never hate you. But now I have to ask you to not hate me for what I'm going to ask you. Can I talk to my mom about you? About the kind of stuff you're going through and how you've been feeling? Because I'm worried. And I care about you and want you to feel better. My mom's a really good therapist. She's helped lots of people.

Love,

Connor

From: yikes!izzy

To: condorboy

Date: Wednesday, December 28—8:03 PM

Subject: Re:

Connor,

Is that really the best you can do? Go running to your mom when I get too difficult to handle? Every fucking email, it's "my mom" this, "my mom" that, like you're fucking in love with her or something. She doesn't even know me. How could she possibly help? Just because you can't figure me out doesn't mean I'm crazy. How could you even say something like that? What the hell is wrong with you? Fuck you and fuck your mom and fuck your stupid dog, too. What kind of stupid name is Señor Cuddlebones? She's not even a boy or Mexican.

Iz

From: condorboy

To: yikes!izzy

Date: Thursday, December 29—10:27 AM

Subject: sorry

Dear Isabel,

I'm sorry. I'm really, really sorry. I didn't realize how upset that would make you. I thought that since my mom is a therapist, maybe she'd have some insight that could help. I guess I just panicked when you started talking about how scared you were, and I didn't know what to do. It scares me when you talk like that. I don't know how to help you. How do you want me to help you?

Love,

Connor

From: yikes!izzy

To: condorboy

Date: Friday, December 30—7:33 PM

Subject: Re: sorry

Connor,

I don't know how I want you to help me. I really don't. I'm sorry I got so mad. Can you swoop down and save me from all the crazy thoughts in my head? Can you do that? God, I'm so tired. But no matter what I do, I can't sleep. I think God is trying to punish me. I must have been a tyrant in my past life. I am so sick of hearing myself think. Tell me a story. Please?

Iz

Friday, December 30—7:34 PM

condorboy: are you there?

yikes!izzy: maybe

condorboy: do you still hate me?

yikes!izzy: no i don't hate you

yikes!izzy: you're just always trying to be so helpful and sometimes it drives me crazy

condorboy: sometimes it seems like you want my help

condorboy: like when you specifically say "help" in an email

yikes!izzy: i don't know what i want

yikes!izzy: tell me a story

condorboy: what kind of story?

yikes!izzy: the entertaining kind

condorboy: happy or sad?

yikes!izzy: either one

yikes!izzy: as long as it's true

yikes!izzy: which i guess means it'll be sad

condorboy: ok

condorboy: stay tuned

yikes!izzy: ok

condorboy: ok

[**yikes!izzy** is offline.]

From: condorboy

To: yikes!izzy

Date: Friday, December 30—10:04 PM

Subject: a sad, true story for a sad, true girl

Dear Isabel,

Okay, you asked for it. Here's probably the saddest true story I know from personal experience. I really don't understand how you expect this to make you feel better, but I have learned it's better not to question you.

Once upon a time, two Christmases ago, instead of our usual day of volunteering at the food bank, my mom decided we'd spend my entire winter break in a little village in Ecuador. At first I was excited, assuming we'd be in some beautiful tropical place on the beach, but that was not the case. We were way up high in the Andes mountains and it was freezing and we had to sleep in a tiny room of a dirt-floor hut, and all we ever got to eat was boiled potatoes and rice and, if we were really lucky, guinea pig. I had a pet guinea pig when I was little. Her name was Hammy and I loved her, so you can imagine it was difficult eating her relatives. Believe me, I wouldn't have done it if I hadn't been so hungry.

My mom thought it was the greatest thing ever, of course, but it was really hard for me to see it that way when I was constantly freezing and starving to death and I read through all the books I brought in the first week. We were volunteering with some organization that builds schools in little villages, so that's pretty much all we did. All day long. We woke up at six thirty to eat boiled potatoes and drink instant coffee. Then we'd work until noon, when we'd stop for a half hour to eat more boiled potatoes, plus some rice and a mysterious stew. Then we'd work until five, have an hour or so before dinner to read or cry or bathe using the freezing-cold spigot outside our hut (the family we lived with was considered rich because of this spigot).

I don't want to sound like an ugly American and just complain about the food and cold water. But that's what I'm doing so far, isn't it? I feel good about the work we did, and the people we met were wonderful. It was an amazing experience, blah blah blah. Fuck, I do sound like an ugly American. Shoot me now.

Really though, it wasn't all hard work and questionable stew. Nights were actually usually pretty fun. The little village we were working in was a couple miles from a larger village that had a big plaza and some restaurants and a couple of bars. My mom would go out for dinner with the other volunteers, and I would wander around town with my host brother, Manuel. He was fifteen and didn't like me very much, but he let me follow him and his friends around while they made fun of each other and whistled at girls. Not much different than here, really. Only instead of smoking pot in the Safeway parking lot, the kids there drank cheap rum in a colonial town square with the snowcapped Andes in the background. It was definitely a much more scenic environment for losing brain cells. I tried to follow along as best I could with my Spanish 3a skills. Basically, they just talked about girls, same as here. Sometimes they asked me about life in the US, but I don't think they were very impressed with my answers. Something I didn't notice until later (and this will become relevant in a second) was that no one ever really talked about their plans for the future. It seems like the only thing anyone ever talks about these days is college and what they're going to major in, where they're going to live and travel, the crap they're going to buy, what they want to be when they grow up. But these guys in Ecuador didn't talk about stuff like that.

I remember the topic of conversation for three nights in a row was this one family's new truck. They owned the most popular restaurant in town, and the truck was brand-new and big and probably the shiniest thing for miles around. The guys were talking about it in this very reverential way, and then one of them said something like "I'm going to get a truck like that someday," and then everyone got real quiet and awkward, like he had just done something totally unacceptable and everyone was too embarrassed to acknowledge it. Finally, someone said *Sí* and everyone else let out a big, relieved breath, and there was nodding all around. And then someone changed the subject to a particular classmate's boobs, and the truck was never mentioned again.

This leads me to the next phase of my story. There was this one guy, Esteban, who I always saw when I went down to the plaza. I think he was nineteen or twenty, and he was almost always drunk when I saw him. He was someone I recognized, but I never actually talked to him until about a week into our stay. I was sitting at the Plaza being ignored as usual by Manuel and his friends, when Esteban came weaving over and sat down right next to me. He exchanged *hola*s with the guys, then they all started back with the previous conversation, except that Esteban didn't want to talk to them, he wanted to talk to me.

He started asking me about school, about what I like to do for fun, what I want to study in college, what I want to be when I grow up, and he kept nodding his head earnestly like I was proving some important theory correct, and even though he was drunk and his eyes couldn't focus too well, he was looking at me with this kind of intensity that was almost scary. At one point he whistled and shook his head. "Art," he said. "You can go to college to study *art*."

When he was done asking questions, he got very serious and almost seemed sober for a minute. "I'm the smartest one for miles around," he said with a big sweep of his arm that knocked over a rum bottle, which he saved with supersonic reflexes before it even spilled a drop. I chuckled for a second until I realized he was totally serious.

"They couldn't believe how smart I was," he continued. "I could do all the math problems without writing anything down." Then he poked me hard in the chest. "You," he said. "Are you good at math?"

"No," I told him.

He nodded and closed his eyes. "Art college," he said, and I waited for him to continue. He just sat there for a while with his eyes closed, not saying anything, swaying a little like the wind was pushing him.

"You come here talking about college," he said, without opening his eyes. "All you nice people who come here to build things. You ask us what we're going to do when we grow up." He opened his eyes and threw his arms out wide. "This is as grown-up as I'm ever going to get."

I remember sitting there and feeling more out of place than

I'd ever felt in my entire life. Like I was doing something shameful just by existing. Esteban must have noticed, because he started patting me on the head like I was a dog or a dumb child, a little harder than was necessary, which I hoped was the result of the alcohol and not hostility. "You're nice people," he said. "All of you, such *nice* people," and I knew he meant all sorts of things by "nice" that I would never understand.

And then he started crying. You'd think being raised by a therapist, I'd be somewhat comfortable with tears. But I don't think anyone can ever really be comfortable with watching someone fall apart in front of them. Even professionals like my mom need an extra glass of wine after a particularly hard day of listening to clients. And there was this man weeping in front of me, the smartest man for miles around, with nowhere to go. I didn't know what to say, so I told him I was sorry. He didn't respond. So I said it again in Spanish. He looked at me almost like he felt sorry for *me*. "Of course you are," he said.

He stood up and held out his hand. I stood up and took it. We shook solemnly, and he said, *"Buena suerte, artista. "* He took his rum bottle and started walking away. After a few steps, he started jogging. And then he started running wildly. A few people turned their heads to watch him, but I suppose they were used to his antics by then and they lost interest pretty quickly. I was the only one still watching as he disappeared into the shadows, and I kept listening until I could no longer hear his footsteps on the cobblestone street.

I think I might have been the last person who saw him before he died.

The next day, things happened pretty much like normal. And that's what I feel worst about. That I didn't wake up thinking about him. That I didn't worry or wonder where he ran off to. We hammered nails all day and ate our boiled potatoes and mystery stew, then I followed Manuel down to the plaza. And that's when I realized something was wrong. No one was laughing. No one was whistling at the group of beautiful girls walking through the plaza. The group of beautiful girls was crying.

Esteban had been found that afternoon, facedown at the bottom of the nearby waterfall. He had taken off his shoes before he jumped, set them neatly at the edge of the cliff.

We went to the funeral. All of the volunteers, even the ones who had never met him, like it was some kind of tourist activity included with the cost of the program. *Muy auténtico.* People wore their $200 hiking boots and fancy Gore-Tex jackets as we walked the solemn procession through town, as we listened to the final, hollow sound of his casket being pushed into the cemetery wall. We saw his pale, puffed body and unrecognizable face as he was laid to rest painted up like a clown, cheap makeup being the local undertaker's only tool to make him presentable to God. And we listened to his mother's screams echoing and trapped between the village's funerary walls. *"M'ijo, mi hijo!"* she wailed. *"Ay, Dios,* why did you take my son?"

There we were at Esteban's funeral, crying along with all his relatives. But it was like we were crying at a movie, like we were using it as some kind of entertainment, like the more we could cry about it, the bigger our egos could get. Like all those times we shuddered at his mom screaming—we could use them to tell ourselves we were a little more human than we were the day before. Maybe my mom could let go of a little of that White Guilt she's always talking about. She could feel satisfied that we saw the "real" country, that we weren't your regular tourists. Then we could go back home to our little utopia and pretend we're saving the world whenever we donate $50 to UNICEF.

It didn't matter that after we left, the volunteers kept coming, continuing the conveyor belt of monthlong stays in the villages. They take day trips to the same waterfall where Esteban was found facedown; they swim in that river, they splash in the cool water and remark how clean it is. They continue to ask the local kids about their plans for the future. They take their photos and tuck them safely away in scrapbooks they'll only open every few years. They have the time of their lives, and then they go home and forget.

Good night, Isabel. I hope your dreams are happier than this.

Love,
Connor

From: yikes!izzy

To: condorboy

Date: Saturday, December 31–1:57 PM

Subject: Re: a sad, true story for a sad, true girl

Dear Connor,

Fuck you. That is the saddest fucking story I've ever heard. But it worked somehow. I must have cried myself to sleep last night. I can't even remember. Real sleep, too. Like straight through the night sleep, twelve whole hours. I don't think I even dreamed. I'm a new woman, and I have you to thank. And Esteban, I suppose. But I don't want to think about him anymore. And I'm sure that makes me an asshole, but I don't care. I'm done with feelings. Tonight is New Year's Eve and I will celebrate the New Year by sleeping through it.

But something's bothering me. Tell me–was I not supposed to cry about him either? Am I a big phony like your mom and all the volunteers who didn't know him? Am I claiming some piece of his life by being moved by it, a piece I am not entitled to? Would it be better if I felt nothing at all? Am I an asshole American for caring?

Is this your big complaint about your mom? That she cried at a stranger's funeral? Yeah, Connor, she's a real monster. Should she have been sad some other way? What's the right way to be sad about it? Would you prefer that she didn't give a shit at all? It's fucking sad, Connor. And let me remind you that I'm supposed to be the cynical one, not you. I don't know, maybe she shouldn't have gone to the funeral. But I think it's admirable that she wants to feel things even if they're uncomfortable. Most people spend their whole lives trying to avoid feeling anything at all.

You complain about it, but this is the best thing she gave you—your ability to feel the stuff everyone else ignores. I think my lack of sleep disrupted my usual flow of snark, but I'm being totally serious. You're not normal, Connor, and I mean that in the nicest way possible. Boys are not supposed to be this sensitive. And this is why I love you.

Love,

Isabel

Dear Isabel,

   What did you mean by "I love you"? Like, I love you like a friend, or I love you like something else?

(Love),

Connor

From: yikes!izzy

To: condorboy

Date: Sunday, January 1–5:49 PM

Subject: Re: question

My dearest Connor,

    Does everything I write have to be dissected and given so much meaning? You should know by now I'm full of shit. Don't ever take anything I say or do seriously.

Isabel

From: condorboy

To: yikes!izzy

Date: Sunday, January 1—8:33 PM

Subject: Re: question

Isabel,

    So you don't love me?

Connor

From: yikes!izzy

To: condorboy

Date: Monday, January 2—9:34 PM

Subject: vitamins

Connor,

Excuse me if I have more pressing things on my mind, but Trevor is arriving tomorrow and I'm freaking out. Even though I'm sleeping again, everything still feels a little rickety, like I'm here but not quite here, like I'm just a stand-in for my real self, like someone could just reach over and pinch me and I'd deflate. I thought I was feeling better, but I don't know anymore. I don't know anything. I used to think I knew exactly who I was, but that was all bullshit. I can't be sure of anything about myself, about what I think or how I feel or if I'm even a good person. I don't know if I want to go to any of the colleges I applied to. I don't know if I want to be with Trevor. I don't know if I want to be a vegetarian anymore. I feel like I'm a snow globe and someone shook me up and now every little piece of me is falling back randomly and nothing is ending up where it used to be.

I wonder if I could have a food allergy. Or if I'm deficient in some kind of vitamin. I've heard wheat allergies can really fuck you up.

Love,

Isabel

From: condorboy

To: yikes!izzy

Date: Tuesday, January 3—7:57 PM

Subject: Re: vitamins

Dear Isabel,

I'm not an expert, but I'm pretty sure wheat allergies don't make you cheat on your boyfriend (even if he is a douchebag). Besides that, I don't know what to tell you. You keep talking about something being wrong, but then you get mad at me when I try to help.

Here's a crazy idea: What if you didn't see Trevor while he's in Seattle? What if you finally got rid of him like you know you should?

Love,

Connor

From: condorboy

To: yikes!izzy

Date: Friday, January 6—11:42 PM

Subject: Re: vitamins

Isabel,

Hello? Are you there? Did I piss you off again? God, I can't figure you out.

Love,

Connor

From: condorboy

To: yikes!izzy

Date: Monday, January 9—5:19 PM

Subject: Re: vitamins

Isabel,

Come on. I hate this.

Connor

From: condorboy

To: yikes!izzy

Date: Wednesday, January 11—9:42 PM

Subject: Re: vitamins

Isabel,

Seriously, I have no idea what I did wrong this time.

Love,

Connor

From: yikes!izzy

To: condorboy

Date: Thursday, January 12—11:12 PM

Subject: officially a loser

Dear Connor,

    Calm down. I'm not mad at you. Just because I'm not waiting by my computer every second of the day doesn't mean I'm mad at you. I have a life, you know. I just happened to be busy being Trevor's whore and getting disowned by my parents and practically committed to a mental institution. L-O-fucking-L. Not funny. But I have to pretend it's funny or else . . . I don't know what else. Pain. Torture. Dismemberment. Definitely heart-break. Humiliation. Doing the same thing over and over and hoping it'll feel different this time, but it never does.

    Even though I'm supposed to be "grounded" indefinitely, I let Trevor talk me into basically running away from home. I left a note and every-thing and said I'll be okay and not to worry, and then I turned my phone off and attempted to switch off my guilt, too. And then I commenced to spend the next four days sleeping on Trevor's friend's couch in Ballard. Yeah, I know, really great use of teenage rebellion. But really, what else did I have to do? Hang out at home and get ignored by my parents? Hang out at school and feel like an alien? At least Trevor sort of pays attention to me, and by "pays attention" I mean "wants to put his penis inside me when we happen to be in the same city." God, I'm pathetic. I call girls pathetic who let themselves get used like this. I'm supposed to think I deserve better, right? I'm supposed to demand what I want? I'm supposed to be a feminist, right? Yes and yes and yes, but I just can't help myself. Feminist FAIL. I want him to want me. I *need* him to want me. Blah, blah, BARF.

The sex was good, if you need to know. That was never the problem. Even though it wasn't the most romantic of situations, at least in those brief moments I was able to get some sort of positive answer for why I was subjecting myself to this torture. But the more I think about it, the less it all seems worth it. Even if those few minutes were mind-blowing, they still occurred on some dude's couch with a guy who has never once asked me how I'm feeling. There were no candles or music or lingering kisses, no cuddling or hand-holding or even really that much conversation. There was just "Oh, James is going to the store for cigarettes, let's fuck," or "James is taking the dog for a walk, take off your pants."

So what do I do as I realize more and more that he doesn't give a shit about me? I ask him if I can come visit him in Portland. Because that's the kind of thing a girl with self-esteem does. She says, "Why don't I skip school and possibly fuck up my chances to get into a good college so I can run away from home (again) to spend a weekend with a guy who hates my guts?" Trevor practically LAUGHED when I suggested it, but I couldn't leave it. I practically started begging, coming up with all kinds of reasons why it was a good idea, like I could tell my parents I'm doing a college visit at Reed and staying in the dorms for the weekend.

Then he said, "You want to go to *Reed*?" like he was terrified, like he never thought such a horrible thing was possible. Then all this bullshit started coming out of his evil little pores, like "Oh, sorry, I'm really busy," and "My roommates don't like having visitors," and "It's not really a good time," and "Are you sure you really want to go to college in Portland?" and "Do you realize how many kids kill themselves at Reed?" and "Wouldn't you rather go to school somewhere farther away, like ANTARCTICA?" and "Do you actually think I want to have a relationship with you, you STUPID, CRAZY GIRL?" Okay, so the last couple he didn't say. He didn't have to.

At first, I thought it was just about him being embarrassed by how young I am. But then I remembered something weird that happened the last time he was in town. We were out at a bar, and all of a sudden he got really weird and said he wanted to leave, and then this guy came up with his girlfriend and they exchanged greetings all pseudopolite but I could tell they sort of hated each other. And Trevor doesn't even introduce me, and the guy goes, "How's Rachel?" and it's obvious he's asking Trevor, but he's looking straight at me, like he's trying to tell me something too. Trevor says, "Fine," and the guy goes, "Who's this?" and Trevor goes, "Let's go," and he starts pulling me toward the door, and as we're leaving I can hear the guy yelling, "Tell Rachel we say hi!"

Of course I asked him about it as soon as we were out the door, and of course he wouldn't tell me anything. All he said was that he used to date a girl named Rachel and the guy was her ex-boyfriend. But I didn't believe him. I tried to pretend I believed him then, but that's when I still had the energy to pretend all sorts of things. I can't do it anymore. I really can't. I think I may finally be thinking clearly. I think I may finally end it with Trevor.

Shit.

My chest feels like it's being torn open. Little dagger feet are stomping around in my heart. Giant claws are reaching in and crushing my rib cage, tearing everything apart until they can get to my lungs, grabbing and squeezing until all the air is gone, until I'm just a bloody, flat, dead thing.

In other news, my parents are finally making me see a shrink. I go on Monday. Are you happy now?

Isabel

From: condorboy

To: yikes!izzy

Date: Friday, January 13—11:03 PM

Subject: Re: officially a loser

Isabel,

No, of course I'm not happy. Why would it make me happy to know you're in pain? I would do anything to relieve it. I would follow you around begging for you to give some of it to me. I am that kind of person. I don't know if that's good or bad. I don't know the difference between kindness and letting people walk all over you. All I know is I want you to be happy, and if I could do anything to give that to you, I would.

You are not a bloody, flat, dead thing. You are in fact quite beautiful.

Love,

Connor

From: yikes!izzy

To: condorboy

Date: Saturday, January 14—12:12 AM

Subject: save me

Dear Connor,

I know what you can do to make me happy: Invite me over next weekend. Take me away from all of this and let me run around in the forest with you. We can build our own little Craft Shack with sticks and stones, we can teach the squirrels and raccoons how to tie-dye, we can lie around in pine needles all day and listen to the wind toss pinecones to the ground. We can lick slugs again. We can do all the things we forgot how to do, all the things our lives won't let us. Just you and me and the deer and the owls.

I'm serious, Connor. I miss you. I miss you so much. I've been living in this world inside my head where all I see are ugly reproductions of myself, except one of them dresses like Trevor, and one of them walks like my sister, and one of them talks like my math teacher, and one of the them smells like my mom, and I can pretend they're all real people, that I'm running around trying to please them, but none of them are actually real. They're just projections of myself and my fears and all the things I wish I did better. You're the only real person I have left, the only one who's something more than a need or a judgment or anger or disappointment. I don't know how to explain it, just that I feel less alive now than I have in a long time, and I know—I just know—you can remind me what it feels like to have someone look at me and love me without wanting me to be something else.

Love,
Isabel

From: condorboy

To: yikes!izzy

Date: Saturday, January 14—1:42 PM

Subject: Re: save me

Dear Isabel,

I may not know how to do much, but I can do that. I can tell you as many times as you need me to that you're enough.

My mom is really excited to meet you. Jeremy is really excited to meet you. Señor Cuddlebones promises to be on her best behavior. The birds and the squirrels and the raccoons and the owls can barely control themselves. And don't even get me started on the deer. Even the bats are freaking out a little, and they're usually too cool to care about anything.

Are you going to drive? I'll need to give you directions because the internet gets people lost here. It's a lot cheaper if you just walk on the ferry, and I can pick you up at the terminal if you tell me what boat you're going to catch. I was thinking we could go for a little hike or something, or hang out at the beach, then maybe hang out with Jeremy, and if there's a party we could go to that, but we totally don't have to if you want to have a low-key time. I'd be perfectly happy just hanging out you and me. And my dog. You really have to meet her. You have to see what I mean about her looking like Robert De Niro. It's unreal. If anyone can appreciate it, you can.

Are you sure your parents will let you come? Shouldn't you be grounded until you're fifty or something?

Love,
Connor

From: yikes!izzy

To: condorboy

Date: Monday, January 16–10:46 PM

Subject: brains

Connor,

You want to read the new play I wrote? It's brilliant. Pulitzer material for sure. It goes like this:

The Therapy Session

By Crazy McCrazyPants

Dr. BigHead: How are you feeling?

Me: Fine.

Dr. BigHead: Is there anything you'd like to talk about?

Me: No.

Dr. BigHead: Would you like to talk about why you're here?

Me: No.

Dr. BigHead: Your father said he and your mother are concerned about your erratic and self-destructive behavior.

Me: . . .

Dr. BigHead: Is there anything you'd like to say about that?

Me: No.

(47 minutes of silence)

Dr. BigHead: It looks like our time is up.

Me: Bye.

The End.

Ta-motherfucking-da. I'm into minimalism these days.

Love,

Isabel

(P.S.: I don't really plan on involving my parents in my decision to come visit you.)

From: condorboy

To: yikes!izzy

Date: Tuesday, January 17—4:27 PM

Subject: Re: brains

Dear Isabel,

I feel like I should tell you to be good and not lie to your parents anymore. But the truth is that my desire to see you is forcing me to ignore my conscience. Is this a case of you being a bad influence on me?

You want to hear something ridiculous? Alice wants to get back together again. Remember her? My lesbian ex-girlfriend? Well, apparently she's lonely being the only out girl at our school (besides Leeza Bonham, who's been out since she was in the womb, but who's horribly ugly and boring), so she thought it would be a good idea for us to "hang out," but only "temporarily" until we can both find "appropriate girlfriends." To be honest, I might have said yes to this arrangement a few days ago. I can imagine myself thinking it wouldn't be too bad to be naked with someone, anyone, even if she was closing her eyes the whole time and telling me not to speak so she could imagine she was with someone of a completely different gender. But I guess things feel different now, like maybe I don't have to settle for stuff I don't actually want. I don't know how much of this has to do with you coming over this weekend, but it definitely has to do with feeling happy and excited, and that definitely has to do with you, which is confusing. You made the rule a long time ago that we weren't allowed to destroy our friendship with trying to be anything more than friends. But I don't think I was being completely honest when I agreed to that. And I'm starting to question why you made that rule in the first place. I don't think you were being completely honest either. You think you're supposed to be with guys like Trevor, but you're not. And I think you're starting to figure that out.

Love,
Connor

From: yikes!izzy

To: condorboy

Date: Tuesday, January 17—11:35 PM

Subject: baby birds

Connor,

    I'm not figuring anything out. Sometimes I think I am, just for a few minutes, then all of a sudden the snow globe gets shaken and everything falls apart again. You think it's so simple. You think everything can be solved by talking about your feelings and being nice to people and being with who you love. But what if talking about your feelings doesn't fix anything? What if what you really need is to make the feelings go away?

    Maybe you're a little too skinny and a little too short, and maybe you're too smart and too talented to fully integrate into this stupid little world, but there's a place for you on the periphery, a place reserved for the people who don't quite fit in but who are allowed to stick around because they make everything a bit more colorful. And maybe you're not like everyone else, but at least you get along with them. At least you know how to smile when you're supposed to and when to say please and thank you. At least you know when to shut up.

Of course the luckiest ones are the people with no consciousness, the ones who have no idea anything is wrong. They keep on with their small lives and don't question what they're for. Even the misfits and the uglies know deep down there's a place for them, even if it isn't at the top, and there's security in that. It may not be glamorous, but it's home.

The thing is, I don't think you know what it feels like to have no home. Yes, I'm being melodramatic. I'm always being melodramatic. But the truth is, I'm an alien. I was born to the wrong family. I was born in the wrong world. I am not built to survive here. Maybe there's some world out there where I'm perfectly adapted. Maybe there's a galaxy with a planet that's just a little more tilted, with a sun that shines just a little bit darker, and that's where I'm supposed to be, where it somehow makes sense to feel this broken.

Do you remember that book from when we were kids, *Are You My Mother?* It's the one with the baby bird whose mom goes out to hunt some worms, except he doesn't know that and the egg cracks open while she's gone and he gets born to an empty nest and he thinks he's an orphan. Heavy shit for a kid's book, right? Anyway, he goes around asking everyone he sees if they're his mother. He knows he's supposed to have one; he has some instinct that's telling him someone's supposed to love him, but he doesn't even know what a mother's supposed to look like. I'm like that stupid little bird, asking everyone I meet if they're my mother—you, Trevor, the bartender at Linda's, the postman, the drag queen who hangs out across the street from my school, this garbage can on the corner—*ARE YOU MY FUCKING MOTHER?* And just like the book, everyone just sends me away.

Do you know the feeling that everything's wrong, that your skin does not belong on your body, that your body does not belong, period? I imagine the world without me, and it doesn't make me sad at all. It doesn't make me feel anything. I could just drift away from my silly little life and make space for someone who truly deserves to be here. And she will rise up from my ashes to take my place, and she will be the kind of daughter my parents could love, she will be the kind of girl Trevor will want to call his girlfriend, and she will be the kind of friend you deserve. She will call you on the phone and swim over to visit. She will brave sharks and killer squids to see you. She will give something back instead of just take, take, take all the time.

I am a parasite on this world. I suck the life out of the things I love. I multiply and spread until I've consumed you. And even when you're gone, even after I've licked up every last crumb of you, I'm still hungry. I'm starving, Connor. I'm empty and lonely and lost and I'm starving, and there isn't enough in the whole wide world that could make me feel whole.

Somebody shoot me. Somebody put me out of my misery. Please.

Love,

Isabel

From: condorboy

To: yikes!izzy

Date: Wednesday, January 18—7:41 PM

Subject: Re: baby birds

Dear Isabel,

Don't you see? Neither of us fits in. That's why we have each other. We can build our own little world full of weird, beautiful things. We can make a new normal, just for us. There are fewer of us, but we exist. And it's pretty amazing if you think about it—we get to create our own reality instead of just accepting the old, used one everyone else gets. We're the lucky ones, Isabel. When are you going to start seeing that?

Love,

Connor

From: yikes!izzy

To: condorboy

Date: Thursday, January 19–12:05 AM

Subject: Re: baby birds

Connor,

    I wish I could believe you, but I can't. I'm not like you. You think I'm this wild and free thing, but I'm not. I'm not free at all.

Isabel

From: condorboy

To: yikes!izzy

Date: Thursday, January 19—5:13 PM

Subject:

You're not coming this weekend, are you?

From: yikes!izzy

To: condorboy

Date: Thursday, January 19—8:08 PM

Subject: Re:

I'm sorry. I'm so tired again. Forgive me.

Isabel,

No. I will not forgive you. I am sick of always forgiving you. It's practically all I do anymore. You promise something, I get excited, then you go crazy and break your promise and I have to pretend it doesn't hurt because I'm afraid that if I tell you how I actually feel, you'll run away even more. You get mad, and I apologize for things I didn't even do wrong. You disappear, and I wait for you to come back. It's always about you, Isabel. Everything is always about you.

You're always talking about what phonies everyone else is, how they're always letting you down, but why don't you look at yourself for a second? You say you're going to do something, and then you don't. That's pretty phony if you ask me. You're the one who's letting someone down. You're the one without integrity. You, Isabel. You're just like everyone you say you hate. For once, just try to follow through on something you say you're going to do, even if it's hard, even if you don't want to. Just try to grow the fuck up.

Connor

From: condorboy

To: yikes!izzy

Date: Saturday, January 21—8:17 AM

Subject: sorry

Isabel,

Shit. I'm sorry. That was harsh. But I meant it.

I wish you were here.

Love,

Connor

From: condorboy

To: yikes!izzy

Date: Monday, January 23—6:09 PM

Subject: sorry part 2

Dear Isabel,

Didn't we always talk about how it was great that we could be so honest with each other? Don't you want me to be able to tell you how I feel?

Love,

Connor

Isabel,

You can't just fucking disappear like this. You're not this selfish. This isn't you. You're the girl who gets a room full of kids to think about art. You're the girl who stops the car so you can pick up litter on the side of the road. Remember that time this summer when those mean girls were picking on that little girl with glasses, and how you made them stop and think about it and apologize, and that girl looked at you like you were a fucking angel, like you saved her life? That's you, Isabel. Not this girl who disappears.

What's happening to you? Talk to me. Let me help you.

Love,

Connor

From: yikes!izzy

To: condorboy

Date: Sunday, January 29—11:58 PM

Subject: Re:

Dear Connor,

   I used to think I was that girl you remember.
And maybe I was, maybe those memories are real,
maybe that girl who looked like me really was an
angel. But maybe angels fall, maybe the wind blows
and just like that they can be twisted into something unrecognizable.

   I don't know what's happening to me. Maybe if
I did, I could fix it. Maybe if I could name it,
if I could say it out loud, it would lose some of
its power.

   Why do you keep writing me back? Why do you keep
wanting to see me? After all I've done, after all
I've not done? Why do you keep putting up with my
shit? What if I can't ever be who you want me to
be? What if I keep letting you down?

Love,

Isabel

From: condorboy

To: yikes!izzy

Date: Monday, January 30—7:01 PM

Subject: Re:

Dear Isabel,

    I don't know the answers to your questions. I don't know if anyone can ever really explain why they believe in someone. But I do. I believe in you. I hope that's worth something.

Love,

Connor

From: yikes!izzy

To: condorboy

Date: Thursday, February 2—9:39 PM

Subject: football

Dear Connor,

The director of my school called my parents yesterday and told them I'm almost failing all of my classes. Needless to say, my parents are not happy. Nothing new. I think there is a limit to the amount of anger and disappointment a person can feel, and if you try to add any more, it just spills out and splatters everywhere. My parents have reached this level, so their reaction to this news barely registered. They just added it to the long list of disappointments that they'll have to get around to feeling eventually.

I'm trying to develop a new technique for dealing with myself. The technique is called "Ignore Isabel." For instance, yesterday afternoon, I started thinking about how maybe some of the crap adults say is actually true, like maybe how well you do in high school really does affect how well you do in college, which does affect the kind of job you get, which does affect how happy you end up being. And maybe the academic disaster that my senior year is turning out to be will create an even bigger disaster in college, and maybe I can't cut it at Reed after all, and maybe I'll have to drop out and I'll never get a degree, and I'll never get a job, and then I'll have to live with my parents for the rest of my life like my sister almost did, except I won't find a nice wife like Karen to save me. The luckiest I'll get is a disgusting old sugar daddy with weird sexual fetishes who I'll have to marry because I could never support myself and it'd be the only way to get out of my parents' house and no one else would want me—but then I decided FUCK THAT, I'm going to force myself to think about something else, so I called my sister. You heard that right, I actually called her on the phone, but she wasn't there, and then I thought about calling you, but that scared me and I chickened out. I can't explain why the phone scares me so much. It just feels unsafe, the way someone can hear you but they can't see you, so it's like they're in control of how they want to interpret your words because you're not there to make sure they're hearing you right, and they can be doing all sorts of weird things and you won't even know about it because you can't see them, and you can't go back and edit everything like you can in email.

So I was standing there in the middle of my room with these bad thoughts waiting there under the surface. I could feel them heating up and getting ready to take over, and I was thinking about how I'm just so sick of it, so sick of myself and my own company, sick enough to think my dad's company would be a better alternative, that WATCHING FOOT-BALL would be a better alternative. That shows you how desperate I am. So I spent the next hour sitting on the floor in front of the couch listening to my dad clap and yell at the little men running around on the screen, and I played about a thousand games of solitaire, and there was something oddly comforting about it, about just wasting my time in the company of someone who doesn't feel the need to talk all the time. When I first showed up, Dad said something like, "To what do I owe this honor?" to which I replied something like, "The rest of the house is infested with poisonous vipers," and then he just allowed me to sit there in silence with him. My dad's not so bad. He's kind of a loser, but he's a nice loser.

You asked me to let you help me. Distract me, Connor. Distract me with all your might.

Now I have something serious to ask you. It's something I've always wondered: Where do guys get skinny jeans?

Love,

Isabel

Dear Isabel,

There's a wise voice inside me that warns against forgiving you so quickly. But I never listen, do I? Señor is giving me that look again, like she's sick of my shit. So am I, but I will continue.

You are asking the wrong guy about skinny jeans, since I vowed long ago to never, under any circumstance, wear them. It's a good question, though. Maybe Jeremy will know. Except he doesn't wear skinny jeans either. Crap, was that totally homo-prejudiced of me to just assume he knows about that kind of thing?

Love,

Connor

Thursday, February 2—10:28 PM

condorboy: hi

yikes!izzy: hi

condorboy: what are you doing?

yikes!izzy: trying to do research for a history paper about the renaissance

yikes!izzy: got distracted by stuff about FURRIES

condorboy: what's "furries"?

yikes!izzy: they're these people who are obsessed with anthropomorphic animals

yikes!izzy: they have conventions where they walk around in animal costumes

yikes!izzy: sometimes there are furry sex orgies where they all hump each other in costume

condorboy: during the renaissance?

yikes!izzy: no, now

condorboy: humans are amazing

yikes!izzy: yes they are

condorboy: i have a question for you

yikes!izzy: uh oh. is it serious?

condorboy: yes. very

yikes!izzy: ok. go

condorboy: what did the hipster say when he walked into the bar?

yikes!izzy: i don't know. what?

condorboy: "let's get out of here, there are too many fucking hipsters"

yikes!izzy: haha! i have to tell that one to my sister

condorboy: i texted jeremy about the skinny jeans question. he doesn't know where guys get skinny jeans either

yikes!izzy: they must all be wearing women's pants

condorboy: yes. most likely.

condorboy: jeremy says hi, by the way. he thinks you've been a dick lately, but he still wants to meet you.

yikes!izzy: tell him i say hi too

yikes!izzy: also, how many hipsters does it take to screw in a lightbulb?

condorboy: how many?

yikes!izzy: it's such a cool number, you've probably never heard of it

condorboy: ha

condorboy: jeremy wants to know when you're coming to visit

yikes!izzy: how many hipsters does it take to flush a toilet?

condorboy: how many?

yikes!izzy: you can't touch that toilet, it's art

condorboy: is that referencing Duchamp's *Fountain*?

yikes!izzy: you are such a hipster for saying that

condorboy: Duchamp was totally a hipster

yikes!izzy: i actually studied for my math test yesterday. i think i did ok.

condorboy: good job!

condorboy: señor cuddlebones caught a squirrel yesterday and buried its bloody carcass under my bed

yikes!izzy: karen's belly is getting really big. she gave me a picture of the ultrasound.

condorboy: alice says she has an internet girlfriend now

yikes!izzy: do you think you ever want to have kids?

condorboy: probably. you?

yikes!izzy: i don't know. i'm afraid i'm too selfish. i'm afraid i'd fuck it up too bad

condorboy: i don't think there's any such thing as a perfect parent. everyone fucks up their kids. that's what builds character or something.

yikes!izzy: hipsters totally don't have kids

condorboy: hipsters eat babies for breakfast

yikes!izzy: hipsters don't eat breakfast. that's how they stay so skinny.

yikes!izzy: your mom seems pretty perfect. she raised you, after all

condorboy: my mom's not perfect

yikes!izzy: this is too much like a real conversation

condorboy: i'm definitely not perfect

[**yikes!izzy** is offline.]

From: condorboy

To: yikes!izzy

Date: Friday, February 3—11:45 PM

Subject: what's the opposite of angst?

Dear Isabel,

You said my mom seems perfect. Yes, she is great, I'll be the first to admit it. Why do I feel so embarrassed saying that? As if liking your parents is something to be ashamed of? Like I'm going to get kicked out of teenage-dom because I enjoy my mom's company?

But she's not perfect, either. Sometimes she drinks too much when she's stressed out, and sometimes she loses her temper and yells for no reason. And she can be really judgmental and mean. For someone who claims to be so tolerant, she can say some really nasty things about people she doesn't agree with. Sometimes I think she's just as prejudiced as the people she calls prejudiced, but she thinks she's right so it doesn't count.

But maybe her hypocrisy is a good thing. Maybe it's taught me to try to be even more honest. Maybe the point of all of our parents' failings is to serve as examples of what not to do. Maybe being a grown-up is all about figuring out how to not become our parents.

In that case, I should become a Republican who hates gay/black/poor/disabled/Muslim/immigrant women and tortures cats and drives a Hummer and eats only genetically modified food full of high-fructose corn syrup and preservatives. I should refuse to go to college because the cult of Higher Education is full of lesbians and commies. I should buy some guns and wear a fur coat and join the military and kill babies in third-world countries while picketing a woman's right to choose. That'll show her.

Sadly, I don't think I have too much to rebel against. Even when she's full of shit, my mom is a pretty decent person, which totally sucks. How can I possibly be an artist without any good angst? But of course we've already gone over this.

Love,

Connor

From: yikes!izzy

To: condorboy

Date: Sunday, February 5—7:01 PM

Subject: Re: what's the opposite of angst?

Dear Connor,

I have angst oozing out of my pores that puddles on the ground. I should mop it up and sell it to nice, well-adjusted kids like you.

My mom started talking to me again. I think it was probably only because Gennifer and Karen came over for dinner last night, but it's still a start. Maybe it's also because my brother ended up in jail again, so she realizes that I'm not all that bad in comparison.

Jesse got caught buying heroin from an undercover cop. He totally wins the award for most-fucked-up member of my family. My mom told us all over dinner, and my sister just put her head in her hands, and Karen said something like, "It's obscene that they're going after the users instead of the dealers," and I think I dropped my fork on the floor. My dad just looked at his plate, sadly shaking his head.

"He's at the King County jail right now," my mom said. "You all can go visit him if you want." She did not say "we." No one said anything. "His attorney is going to try to get the judge to order him to go to rehab instead of getting jail time." Karen sat there nodding, and Gennifer was shaking her head, and for some reason I started crying, and no one even seemed to notice. I don't know why. I wasn't feeling particularly emotional, and then all of a sudden I saw Jesse on the floor like I found him when I was little, saw him lying in the hospital bed with tubes in his arms. And then I started thinking about before he was like that, when he was just a normal, pimply fourteen-year-old who no one really worried about. That's the weirdest part—he was just so *normal*, like he got Bs in school, never really got in trouble, had a few friends he did things with. Then it was like, all of a sudden when he was around my age, something just broke. All of a sudden, everything seemed to piss him off and he would walk around in these rages all the time. And then he just started hiding from everyone, which I guess is when he started doing drugs. I started thinking about how my grandmother killed herself before I was born, how my mom is such a perfectionist it's impossible for her to feel joy, then of course there's my brother, and then it just hit me—my family is cursed. It's written into my DNA to self-destruct.

I got up and went to the bathroom and tried to distract myself long enough to stop crying. But every time I thought I was getting a handle on things, I'd start thinking about my brother when he was around twelve and I was six and he'd humor me by coming to my stupid tea parties, and he was always so patient, and he'd even make his voice all high and pretend to talk for my stuffed animals, and he'd compliment the invisible tea and say what a wonderful time he was having. That was a different person from the guy who's in jail right now. And what does that mean about how I'm going to turn out? How different am I going to be from that girl you knew this summer? You may have been the last person to see her.

I was able to get my shit together enough to sit through the rest of dinner. My sister kept looking at me and raising her eyebrows and telepathically asking me what's wrong, but I'd just smile and mouth that everything was fine. The subject got changed to what they're doing to prepare for the baby, which is something everyone can agree is a lovely topic of conversation. We're so tragically modern. Or would it be postmodern? Jesus, Isabel, shut up.

I spent the rest of the evening lying on the roof in my sleeping bag. Did you realize there was a meteor shower last night? A big, cosmic rock pile collided with our atmosphere. It's kind of sad how something that seems so magical is actually a bunch of burning garbage hurtling through space. Luckily I didn't realize that until afterward, when I looked it up. That night, I was still pleasantly naive. I could still get excited about burning space garbage. I could believe it was a bunch of shooting stars. I could believe it was something to wish on. Every couple of minutes, I'd see one, but it was always just out of my vision. I would only ever just barely catch some movement out of the corner of my eye, but by the time I shifted my focus, the star would already be gone. I have never seen a shooting star straight-on, never fully in focus. It's like I've always just missed them. And I guess that's just the nature of them, because space is a such a big place, and it's impossible to know where to look.

Love,
Isabel

From: condorboy

To: yikes!izzy

Date: Monday, February 6—8:33 PM

Subject: Re: what's the opposite of angst?

Dear Isabel,

Señor and I were watching that same meteor shower! I was wondering what it would feel like to fall like that, so fast you catch on fire, so perfectly out of control. I was thinking about how I've never really been out of control like that. I've been supported and cared for and accepted. I've never been in any kind of real danger. I should feel grateful for that, and I am. But I also feel like I'm missing something, like there's some essential part of being human that I don't have. All day long, I'm surrounded by kids complaining about something—their parents, their curfew, their chores, their college applications—and it all seems so ridiculous, these problems of abundance. The real problems are the things people don't complain about, the things they keep secret. The things that are so scary, you can't even say them out loud.

I'm scared of getting to the end of this world and realizing it was all a waste of time, that *I* was a waste of time. That's my fear. That's the thing I don't talk about.

Why wouldn't you cry, Isabel? Why wouldn't you be devastated to lose your brother like you have? You talk like emotions are a dangerous thing. What are you so afraid of?

Love,

Connor

From: yikes!izzy

To: condorboy

Date: Wednesday, February 8—11:43 PM

Subject: more useless information

Top 5 People I Want to Have Sex With

5. The barista at Bauhaus coffeeshop
   with the lip piercing
4. Matt Berninger, lead singer of The
   National
3. Banksy, even though I don't know what
   he looks like
2. Michael Cera
1. Pink

From: condorboy

To: yikes!izzy

Date: Thursday, February 9—10:10 PM

Subject: Re: more useless information

Dear Isabel,

Well, I don't know this barista you speak of. Matt Berninger and Banksy, I guess I can understand, although Mr. Berninger is like eight feet tall and Banksy supposedly looks like a chubby, middle-aged janitor. But the other two? Michael Cera? That guy is such a wimp. I thought you liked the burly, tattooed guys anyway. And Pink? Last I checked, she's a girl. I thought you didn't roll like that, although of course it's totally okay with me if you do. And she could definitely kick Michael Cera's ass.

Love,

Connor

From: yikes!izzy

To: condorboy

Date: Friday, February 10—12:36 AM

Subject: Re: more useless information

Connor,

I know Michael Cera doesn't seem like my type, but something about him is so freakishly adorable. It's like he puts a spell on me and all of a sudden I hear birds chirping and little rabbits start hopping around and I want to hold him against my breast and let him compliment me and tell me how he's had a crush on me since fifth grade. And I know you're going to hate me for this, but if there was a movie made about us, Michael Cera would totally play you. No question about it.

Pink is fucking hot. It doesn't matter that she's a girl, or that she's a little old, or even that I don't particularly like her music. She is beyond gender. She is beyond mainstream music. She has reached a level of hotness that is even beyond the human species. She could totally kick everyone's ass. She's kind of the opposite of Michael

Cera, when you think about it. Michael Cera's the
kind of person you want to cuddle with. Pink is the
kind of person you want to ravage you.

Isabel

Dear Isabel,

 I don't want Michael Cera or Pink to do anything to me, thank you very much.

Love,

Connor

From: yikes!izzy

To: condorboy

Date: Tuesday, February 14—2:07 AM

Subject: SLUGS!

Connor,

I just had the best idea! Seriously, in my short life full of brilliant ideas, this one is up there, the top of the top, the cream of the crop. Which brings up the important question: What does "cream of the crop" actually mean? What do crops have to do with cream, or any dairy product, for that matter? This is assuming "crop" refers to some kind of plant material. The only other definition I can think of is riding crop, but that makes even less sense. I suppose I could look it up, but I don't have time for that right now.

I have found us a mission, and if you're brave enough to take it—well, let's just say you'd have bragging material for the rest of your life. You know the radio station KUTE? *"Ninety-six point three—The Way You Wanna Be"*? What idiot marketing person came up with that slogan? "The Way You

Wanna Be"? Couldn't they think of anything better to rhyme with "three"? What about "please"? That kind of rhymes. *Ninety-six point three-Give Us Money, Please.* Or *Ninety-six point three-Rich White People Ski.* The possibilities are endless.

I know you must have heard of that big stupid concert they're putting on this weekend, the "Escape to Winter Wonderland" pop music barf-fest, with an impressive lineup of scantily-clad anorexics with boob jobs who can't even sing, committing the crime of spreading poisonous music throughout western Washington. We cannot stand for this! Something must be done! That is why I am calling for your help. Musical integrity needs us. The taste of our generation needs us. We can't let them down. We cannot pass up this opportunity to show the world our ninja skills. Hear that, Connor? You are a NINJA! Don't you dare forget it. The world needs its ninjas desperately. We are a dying breed. Better yet, we are ninjas with a very special knowledge of slugs and other things slimy. You can do a lot of damage with a slug. Imagine those little top-heavy pop kittens getting a face full of slugs. Imagine the chaos that would ensue. There'd be a riot. The riot would turn into a revolution. The revolution would turn into us TAKING OVER THE WORLD.

This is the plan: I come over to Bainbridge and we get all of your mom's reusable hemp grocery bags or whatever, then spend the whole day scouring the woods for slugs. They can survive in a bag overnight, can't they? We'll spray them with water and throw in some croutons or something. We'll have an arsenal of ten or so bags full of slugs. People talk about biological warfare. Well, THIS IS BIOLOGICAL WARFARE. We'll get backstage somehow, using our ninja skills of deception, and we'll find the place where all the costumes are kept. Shoes are an excellent place to hide slugs, Connor. Stuffed inside the legs of pantyhose. Tucked in between the folds of various garments. Nestled in the cups of their oversize bras. In hats and sleeves and legs and every single nook and cranny they could possibly poke their teensy-weensy emaciated body parts into. In their purses and makeup bags and anywhere else slugs can hide. And IN THEIR FREAKING WATER BOTTLES. Those bitches will lose their minds.

So are you with me or ARE YOU WITH ME?

ONWARD!

Iz

From: condorboy

To: yikes!izzy

Date: Tuesday, February 14—8:54 PM

Subject: Re: SLUGS!

Dear Isabel,

Please stop yelling! Slugs? Um, I guess I'm happy to hear that you're excited about something. But have you been hitting the coffee a little too hard lately?

I would love to get arrested with you this weekend, but I'm actually busy. Don't fall out of your chair in surprise, but yes, I have plans. Nothing exciting, just college visits at Evergreen State and Reed, but I'm looking forward to it. Jeremy's coming with me and we're going to be gone until Wednesday. I know he's just humoring me about Evergreen since he's determined to go to a "good school," whatever that means. And Reed has great science, and it's prestigious, and there's a good music scene and queer culture in Portland. And I guess that's all important, but mostly I'm just looking for somewhere I can be weird and do my own thing, maybe get a degree that's potentially useful for getting a job as a teacher or something, not to mention the fact that I probably couldn't get into Reed if I tried. He's more interested in Reed, and I'm more interested in

Evergreen, and we're both just excited to be on our own for the weekend, so I think it's going to be a fun trip. What about you? Do you have anything fun planned for the weekend?

Love,
Connor

From: yikes!izzy

To: condorboy

Date: Wednesday, February 15—11:58 PM

Subject: Re: SLUGS!

What about you? Do you have anything fun planned for the weekend? Jesus, Connor. When did you get so boring? Anyway, you know the answer to that. No, I don't have anything fun planned for the weekend. When do I ever have anything fun planned for the weekend?

Maybe I'll become friends with your beloved Jeremy at Reed next year, and I'll steal him away from you and he'll become my drunken make-out buddy instead of yours, and we'll start a gang with our cool Portland friends and we'll declare war against your lame Olympia friends, and we'll kill you with our top-rate academics while you twitch in the death throes of your wimpy, non-graded classes.

Iz

From: condorboy

To: yikes!izzy

Date: Saturday, February 18—11:07 AM

Subject: Re: SLUGS!

Isabel,

I'm leaving for my trip right now. Do you have any idea how mean your last email sounded? I know you have a sarcastic sense of humor, and usually I find it pretty funny, but I feel like your last email crossed the line into bitch territory. To be honest, my feelings were a little hurt. I just wanted to tell you that.

I also wanted to tell you that I'll probably be away from email for the next few days while I'm on my trip, so don't freak out and think I'm giving you the silent treatment or anything.

Connor

You and your fucking "I" statements! Sometimes it makes me sick how well-adjusted you are. Are there support groups for people raised by therapists? Sorry I was mean. Sorry I am mean. Sorry for all of my fucking faults that seem to have no end. It's like I have no control over it sometimes. These bitchy things just come out and I won't even know about it until I realize someone's pissed off at me. It feels like everyone's pissed off at me right now. I guess I've been saying a lot of bitchy things lately, but the fucked-up thing is I don't even know what they were.

Have you noticed I'm not yelling? I'm trying really hard to stay calm. See? I try, I really do. But it never seems to matter. It's such hard work lately for me to just try to be a normal person, let alone try to be better than normal, which you obviously are and which you deserve and expect me to be, but I can never be no matter how hard I try.

So you want honesty? Okay, here's the deal. I think I'm a little jealous of Jeremy. There, I said it. It seems so stupid and childish, but I guess I feel mad sometimes because I don't have a Jeremy and you do. You're one of those people who people like, and you have a Jeremy, and even though you're a little weird and artsy, the kids at your school seem to think you're one of them to some extent. You're surrounded by real, live people every day who are glad or at least not pissed off that you exist. That must be nice. I try to imagine what it feels like, but I honestly can't. I don't know what it feels like to have a parent who seems genuinely glad you're her kid, teachers and classmates who don't look at you like they wish you'd just drop out already and save them the trouble of dealing with you for the rest of the school year. Wah, wah, wah. I turn into such a whiner when I feel hyper. I think you're right about me drinking too much coffee. Maybe I should cut down. Yeah right, like that's going to happen.

I hope you have a good time down south and all that jazz. I'll just be sitting here trying not to explode all weekend. Don't let Jeremy take advantage of you, and don't let those frisky coeds slip anything into your drink. Hey, I just thought of something! If I go to Reed and you go to Evergreen, we'll only be like an hour away from each other! Not that we're much farther away from each other now, but something about a body of water makes it seem like you're in another world.

Love,

Iz

From: yikes!izzy

To: condorboy

Date: Sunday, February 19–10:18 PM

Subject: boys

Dear Connor,

I know you're on the road and everything, but I'm bored and have no one to talk to, so I'm just going to pretend you're there, okay?

My brother's in rehab. Again. He went once after that time he OD'ed in high school, but I don't think anyone really expected it to work. But this time, I don't know. It can't *not* work. There's nowhere else for Jesse to go except prison or dead. Prison is probably where he should be right now, but for some reason the judge took pity on him and sent him to a six-month in-patient treatment program up in the mountains where even someone smart like Jesse can't find a way to get drugs. We can start visiting after his first month is over, so that's good, I guess. I'm trying not to get my hopes up too much, because we all know how that usually turns out. The truth is, him being up in the mountains doesn't even seem that different than when he lived in Seattle. Even though he's technically been living in the same city as me for all these years, it feels like he's been gone a long time.

What else is going on with me . . . Well, Trevor emailed me yesterday. He didn't even mention the fact that I haven't emailed or texted or called him for the last few weeks, even though that was one of the hardest things I've ever done. I wanted some kind of recognition for it, you know? Like maybe he missed me or his feelings were hurt or he at least wondered why I wasn't contacting him. But apparently he didn't even notice. Fucking asshole. I'm done with men. Seriously. I wish I could be a lesbian like my sister. Then I could find a nice lady like Karen to shack up with and she'd never treat me bad or take me for granted. She wouldn't email me after two months and be like, "Hey, I'm driving through Seattle tomorrow on my way to Vancouver, wanna meet up for a couple hours?" Translation: "Will you be my on-the-road booty call?" The answer is

NO. I didn't even write him back. I deleted his email. He is dead to me.

Aren't you proud of me?

Love,

Iz

From: yikes!izzy

To: condorboy

Date: Monday, February 20—6:46 PM

Subject: puppets

Dear Connor,

Things are speeding up and something tells me I'm supposed to be scared, it's telling me to BE REASONABLE, ISABEL, but it's my mother's voice, not mine. It's my mother's voice stolen into my skull, an earwig or some other kind of creeper crawled in through my ear and lodged in my brain, a whispering parasite saying, DO THIS, DO THAT, but I won't listen. How did she get in there? How do our parents slither inside us and take control like that without our permission? Who gave them that right? Was it God? Did God say go ahead and play your children like puppets? Did God say we don't know better? FUCK GOD. He tells me to be reasonable, calm down, BEHAVE, because maybe then everyone at school wouldn't hate me and maybe I'd actually have friends and maybe my teachers wouldn't make me sit outside because I'm fidgeting and talking too much, maybe everyone wouldn't roll their eyes when I walk by and whisper their little evil spells in my direction. Maybe my sister would call me back, maybe Karen would let me touch her belly longer so I can feel the baby kick. Maybe she wouldn't think I'm poison. Maybe she wouldn't have said, "That's enough," and when I didn't move my hand she said, "THAT'S ENOUGH, ISABEL," like I stung her, but I was just trying to feel the baby, I was just trying to love him, that's all I'm ever trying to do, but she backed away and my sister said, "CALM DOWN, ISABEL," and I kept trying to tell them I didn't mean anything by it, I just wanted to feel the baby, everybody else got to feel the baby but I couldn't feel him, he wasn't kicking for me, just let me see if he'll kick for me. I said just let me try one more time and she said, "THAT'S ENOUGH, ISABEL," again, and she could just say it over and over and it would never get through my thick skull because I'm always wanting and wanting because nothing is ever enough you are never enough I am never enough I am never enough I AM NEVER ENOUGH.

Iz

From: yikes!izzy

To: condorboy

Date: Monday, February 20—6:48 PM

Subject:

Fuck, I'm yelling again. Sorry. I CAN'T DO ANY-
THING RIGHT.

I can't sleep again, but it's a good thing because now I can stay up all night and work on my art, which I've been neglecting because of trying to do my FUCKING SCHOOLWORK because everyone was trying to make me feel guilty about my grades dropping. And I believed them; I let their little jabs of shame get inside me and distract me from what's really important. Does Calculus feed anyone's soul? Do mathematicians feel enlightened when they figure out some stupid equation? I don't know, I am not a mathematician. I AM AN ARTIST. I am a stupid, confused teenager, but I am also an artist, and I have a right to call myself that even though the only galleries I've shown at are my bedroom and my sister's condo. But maybe art isn't about who sees it, maybe all that matters is me and the thing I make, me and the act of creating, those few moments stuck together where you're elevated above this pathetic, polluted world, when you're

covered in paint or plaster and you're talking
to God with your hands and eyes and your big,
pounding heart saying all the things you've ever
needed to say, the movement, THE INTENTION your
only language, and it's bigger than words, bigger than your mouth forming recycled sentences and
exclamations and all those sad, repeated things.
There is only value in the things that have never
existed before. This canvas with these strokes and
these colors and these textures HAS NEVER EXISTED
BEFORE. YOU and ME and THIS are the only things
that matter.

Iz

From: yikes!izzy

To: condorboy

Date: Tuesday, February 21–1:08 AM

Subject: suck

It's not right. None of this is turning out right. It was and then it wasn't and I don't know where the line was drawn and I don't know who drew it. All I know is everything has fallen apart. Everything is upside down and tangled and everything I do just makes it worse, all my attempts to clean up the mess end up spilling and ripping and crushing it to pieces until it's nothing but garbage, all my hard work and heart turned into garbage, and nothing I wanted to say got said, nothing I saw inside got out, and all I'm left with are slivers of something that could have been wonderful but ended up the OPPOSITE of wonderful and now I don't know what to do. I'm awake and covered with paint and I don't want to leave my room because someone will try to talk to me but I have to pee and I haven't eaten all day and why is it always so hard to make something special happen?

Iz

From: yikes!izzy

To: condorboy

Date: Tuesday, February 21—4:27AM

Subject: doppelganger

Connor,

I have an evil twin. She looks just like me and goes around and does bad things and gets me in trouble. She gets mad and breaks my paintbrushes and calls me a failure. She climbs onto the roof carrying all of my disasters. She doesn't care that it's three in the morning. She doesn't care that her hair is wild like Medusa's, that she's been wearing the same ratty pajama pants for two days. She doesn't care that it has started to snow, that the little flakes are sticking to the frozen grass two stories beneath her. She's in a tank top but she can't feel cold. She spits at the snowflakes, at their legendary uniqueness, at their promise that no two are alike. FUCK YOU, she says to the snowflakes. FUCK YOU, she says to everything that's supposed to be special and unique and one of a kind. She spits and her spit becomes just another snowflake, just another frozen wetness on the ground.

The girl has a lighter. I don't know why she has a lighter. Maybe she smokes to spite me, because she knows it is something I would never do. Even with the sky full of big, goofy snowflakes, lighters make fire and fire reduces garbage to ash and at least ash can be useful. So the girl makes fire with the garbage, with the ripped canvas and the broken brushes still wet with paint. Who cares about what I intended? Who cares about what that garbage could have been if nimbler hands had touched it? This girl, my evil twin, she is the true artist. She can harness fire and make it do her bidding. What good is paint against something like that?

Did you know bad art burns hotter than anything? It is true. I felt it. I felt my face turn orange with the reflection, I felt my lips chap and my hands blister, I felt everything destruction feels like before the sirens tore the sky apart, before the spinning lights of danger unplugged all the electricity and left us with garbage again.

And that's when she left, of course—my evil twin, that bitch. Just in time for trouble, she was gone, and there I was, on the roof with the lighter in my hand and the bathrobed neighbor pointing, the policeman saying something I couldn't hear, my mom my dad everyone saying things I couldn't hear. I could not tell them about the girl because I knew they would never believe me. So I came down like they told me. I handed over the lighter and the charred remains of something dead that I had wanted to be beautiful.

Love,

Iz

From: yikes!izzy

To: condorboy

Date: Tuesday, February 21—7:16 AM

Subject: donuts

Dear Connor,

So have you and Jeremy consummated your love yet? Have you met any sexy college girls? Have you been to any wild parties? I know you're on the road and everything, but don't you have one of those fancy phones with internet? Can't you borrow someone's laptop for a couple minutes to write me a quick note reminding me I'm not alone in the world? I'm at a point where I might even be desperate enough to CALL YOU ON THE PHONE, except, if I remember correctly, I refused to take your number when you offered it to me so many months ago.

Don't worry, I'm not going to jail just yet. White girls in good neighborhoods can get away with murder these days. All that happens is they get sent to their room to clean up the wreckage (we must keep up appearances, yesyesyes) while the parental units drink organic free-trade coffee with the policeman downstairs. I wonder if he can taste the difference. Do Seattle cops have better taste in coffee? Do they like donuts as much as people say? Or would it be scones here? Croissants? Something fancier? What do cops in Beverly Hills eat? Do they even *have* donuts in Beverly Hills?

The cop told my parents to be stricter about making me see the shrink. And to make me take a drug test. Ha! In the history of teenagers taking drug tests, I will be the first one that comes out legitimately clean! It'll be all over the news. I'll be a hero to kids everywhere. Maybe the assholes at school will actually start talking to me. No, let's not go too far.

My mom says she doesn't know what to do with me. So I said, "Why do you have to do anything with me?" Then I had to go back to my room. It's funny how they think it's a punishment to be alone in my room with all my beloved stuff, when really that's the only place I can stand to be in this cruel, horrible world. A real punishment would be making me hang out with them all day. But I guess that would be torture for them, too, so I don't expect anyone to suggest that option anytime soon.

I don't think I can keep this up much longer.

But it's like I don't even have a choice. I wish there was a switch that could just turn me off for a little while, let me recharge. LET ME SLEEP. Do you have any idea how that feels? To be soooooooo tired but no matter what you do, you can't sleep? When I die and go to hell, that's what it's going to be like: Hanging out with my parents and having to do math homework and not being able to sleep.

I wish you were here to sing me lullabies.

Love,

Iz

From: yikes!izzy

To: condorboy

Date: Wednesday, February 22—12:22 PM

Subject:

Shit. ShitshitshitshitshitshitSHIT. Every time I think things couldn't possibly get any worse, I am proven wrong, I get a big, fat reminder saying, ISABEL, YOU'RE DOOMED. How could you possibly think you have anything good to hold on to? A sister you can trust? BULLSHIT. Now she's the enemy too. Now she's on their side, with her tricky *Do you want to come over, Isabel? Do you want to have dinner with me and Karen tonight?* And I naively think they're asking because they're the last two people on earth besides you who don't hate me. I think maybe I can go over there and feel some peace for a second. Maybe I can sit on their couch and drink some tea and watch a movie and feel for a couple hours like the world isn't falling apart and that maybe I have a place in it. But I'm asking too much. I AM ALWAYS ASKING TOO MUCH. And I'm sorry I'm yelling again but I can't help it because NO ONE EVER LISTENS TO ME and you're not listening to me, you're probably off in the woods doing Ecstasy with some hot college girl who's giving you a massage while she purrs about how reading Derrida has changed her life, and these words I'm writing are just going to some sad, mysterious place where unread emails go to die.

She's on their side now. My beloved sister has forsaken me too. It was all planned and choreographed and scripted and rehearsed like some crappy reality show where the only point is to humiliate some dumb, unsuspecting schmuck who doesn't know what's coming. And everyone watching at home is laughing their pants off, everyone's making bets on what's going to happen when she finds out she's been punked and then totally loses it on national television. Will she start crying? Will she scream? Will she get violent? Will she become still and silent and slowly quiver her way into a straightjacket?

Just so you know, if you ever want to be COMPLETELY DEAD TO ME, all you have to say are these simple words: "Mom wanted me to talk to you." That's all you need to say to assure me you've officially become the enemy, that you're doing her bidding and you've conspired behind my back. All you have to do is feed me spaghetti and wait until I'm sufficiently full and sleepy, then sit me down on the couch and say, "I have something I want to talk to you about." And you want to know the saddest part? You want to know the part that'll just make you cringe? For a second, my stomach flipped and I got a little tingly feeling in my skin, and I smiled, I actually smiled, because do you know what I thought she was going to say? DO YOU HAVE ANY IDEA? For a brief second before she became a traitor, I actually believed my sister was about to ask me to be her baby's godmother. How incredibly pathetic is that?

Karen was in the kitchen doing the dishes and there we were, sitting in the living room, me with a stupid grin on my face because I had no idea I was about to be thrown under the bus. I was trying to hide how excited I was, preparing to stay calm after she popped the question. But as she opened her mouth, I saw it. I saw the look on her face that said she was scared, that this was not going to be good news, that she was about to break my heart. And then she said it. "Mom wanted me to talk to you." And I only heard snippets of what she said after that, words and phrases like daggers one after another after another after another.

You've been acting strange, Isabel. Your behavior has been erratic. Problems at school. The stunt with the fire. The cops. Is it drugs, Isabel? You can tell me if it's drugs. We can get you help. Why don't you let us help you?

Us. She said US. She is in a unit with them now. US is not me and her anymore. Us means THEM now. And I've been thrown into the category with my brother. They think I'm as bad as the heroin addict locked up in the mountains.

So I left. I just grabbed my stuff and walked out the door. Gennifer tried to stop me, kept trying to tell me she loved me and was trying to help, but all her words bounced off of me. Karen came in and said, "Where are you going?" and I just shrugged. Where could I go? I wasn't allowed to go anywhere except school and home and my sister's condo, and now I only had two of those places left. My world is getting smaller and smaller, and pretty soon I'll lose everything, I'll destroy every single thing I have until all I'll have is a rock to stand on, a little speck of dirt, and then even that will disintegrate and I'll be left with nothing.

They kept talking and I kept leaving, and I could hear Gennifer getting on the phone to call my parents, her new allies, and I walked out the door and shut it calmly behind me and got in my car and put on my seat belt and drove the ten minutes home clenching every muscle in my body, and I think I was breathing, I must have been breathing, but I don't remember there being any air, any movement inside me. I pulled up out-side my house and got out and locked the door and walked inside and didn't even look at my parents who were standing in the living room waiting for me, didn't raise my head to look them in the eyes, barely heard their "Your sister was worried about you. She didn't think you were coming home. Isabel. Talk to us. Isabel. Where are you going?"

and I just went where I always go, to my little box where I don't bother anyone. And as soon as I closed the door behind me, all the sounds and pain I'd been avoiding came rushing out of me and I couldn't hold on anymore, I couldn't hold on, and I melted onto the ground and everything came out, the air and tears and pain and heartbreak, and it sounded like something deflating, it sounded like Esteban's mother in Ecuador, screaming at God for taking the only good thing she had left in this empty, dirty world.

I don't know how long I stayed on the floor like that, how loud I was crying, if my mouth was forming words or sentences, if anyone came in or out or tried to soothe me. All I know is I woke up covered with a blanket and with a pillow under my head, with my throat sore and my eyes puffy and stinging, bruises on the palms of my hands where my nails dug in. There was a bottle of water, a glass of juice, a banana and a muffin sitting on my desk. I am trying to eat the banana as I type this to you. But every time I try to swallow I feel like I'm going to throw up. And something about that just seems so devastating, the fact that I can't even feed myself, that my body hates me so much it doesn't even want to let me eat.

Connor, please write me back. I just need to know you still exist.

Love,

Iz

From: yikes!izzy

To: condorboy

Date: Wednesday, February 22—2:46 PM

Subject:

It's Wednesday, Connor. You're supposed to be back by now. Did the forest swallow you up? Are you turning into wood, into rock, into pine needles? Are you scattered across the forest floor, softening the deer's hoofbeats?

Connor? Are you there?

From: yikes!izzy

To: condorboy

Date: Wednesday, February 22—4:40 PM

Subject:

Please?

From: yikes!izzy

To: condorboy

Date: Wednesday, February 22—8:19 PM

Subject:

Connor, I need you.

From: yikes!izzy

To: condorboy

Date: Wednesday, February 22—11:17 PM

Subject:

She is winning, Connor. My evil twin. I don't know where the real me stops and she begins. She runs and runs and I follow, and it's getting easier, this racing around. The track is part of my feet, her feet. I am strangely calm. I am focused. Everything is clear all of a sudden. The pain comes from the struggle, not from the girl. She wants me to stop fighting. She promises me there will be no conflict. She whispers and her voice is soft. It is not the sound of evil. She says, *Let go*. She says, *Relax*. She says, *Don't you want to stop fighting?* And I say yes. She says, *Close your eyes*. And I do. Then she takes over and I feel myself slipping, and the falling feels like freedom.

From: condorboy

To: yikes!izzy

Date: Thursday, February 23—4:43 PM

Subject: Re:

Dear Isabel,

I'm home now. I was so excited to turn on my computer and write to you about what a great time I had on my trip. But now there's this. There are pages and pages of your fear and pain and paranoia for me to sift through and try to answer.

Isabel, you're scaring me. This isn't just part of your lovable eccentricity anymore. Something is really wrong, and I don't know how to help you. Maybe your sister went about it the wrong way, but she really was trying to help. She's not the enemy and neither are your parents. They may not understand you, but they love you the only way they know how.

Fuck, I feel like whatever I'm going to say is going to piss you off. Anything I want to tell you is going to be taken the wrong way and you're going to make me a villain like you've done to everyone else. I love you, Isabel. So please hold on to that when I tell you I think you need help. Professional help. Whatever's going on is too big for us to handle. It is bigger than me and your sister and your parents. It's bigger than school and Trevor and your art. It is bigger than you, Isabel. It is so much bigger than you.

Don't listen to her. Don't give yourself to whatever sickness is posing as your evil twin. The softness of her voice is all part of the trick. Please. Try to believe me. And please don't hate me for wanting to help you.

Isabel, I want to talk to my mom about this. I want her to talk to your parents. Will you let me do this for you? It seems so wrong to be asking your permission to save you. But I know how you are, and I know you would never forgive me if I contacted your parents behind your back. Fuck, Isabel. Look at the kind of choices you're forcing me to make.

All of my love,
Connor

From: yikes!izzy

To: condorboy

Date: Thursday, February 23–7:09 PM

Subject: Re:

My head is on fire. The flames lick me from the inside. You may think this hurts, but it does not. Just the opposite. Trust me.

Now that you're back, I don't know what I want to say to you.

Iz

Answer my fucking question for once. Please. Let's ask for help.

Do you want to fuck me, Connor? Is that it? Is that what this has always been about? Our so-called friendship, your little sensitive-boy routine, all your understanding and kind supportive words, ALL OF IT just an act to get in my cheap insides. And now you think if you get my parents on your side, I'll have no choice. It'll be like some kind of arranged marriage. You'll be the nice guy who simultaneously betrays and saves me. You will prove yourself worthy to all the assholes who think they know what's best for me. I thought you were better than that I thought you were on my side. But you want to use me like everyone else does and that makes you even worse than Trevor because at least he doesn't pretend to be anything besides an asshole at least he doesn't pretend to want anything more than my body. Yours is the worst kind of dishonesty you made me trust you and you made me start thinking that maybe there's a place in my life for a nice guy maybe there's a nice place in his nice world for me maybe we can just run off and be nice together. These were the things I was thinking Connor. I didn't tell you but I was going to I was going to tell you with the slugs I was going to tell you in the forest I was going to kiss you I had it all planned out I was going to tell you I was starting to wonder if maybe I could let you love me I was going to tell you I painted an island for us. But that's gone now. There is no island and there is no love. You are not the boy I met in the forest you are not the words that soothed me to sleep you are not the heart I thought lived in this machine. I will tear up the canvas until the island is trash like everything else I will burn it on the roof until the cops come again. I will hold out my wrists and ask them to take me. Because what's the use in try- ing to be free if you can't tell a lie from the truth? What kind of freedom is that? What are you supposed to do when you find out the only people you ever loved aren't the people you thought they were? Yes, I loved you, Connor. I always did. But that is irrelevant now because there is no you left, not the you I loved. He never existed. There is only this imposter, this fake, yet another who wants nothing more than to conquer me.

Iz

Isabel,

I loved you the moment I met you and I know you've always known that. But this isn't the you I fell in love with. This isn't the brilliant, funny girl who could make kids believe in magic. I want her back. I want you, the real you, not this evil twin. I want to meet you in the forest and I want to go slug hunting and I want to hold you and make you believe you are safe. I will build us a boat with my bare hands and we will sail to this island in your painting. I will feed you coconuts and all the sweet things I can find. But I can't do this unless you let me help you. Please, Isabel. We can't fix this by ourselves.

Love,

Connor

From: yikes!izzy

To: condorboy

Date: Friday, February 24—5:09 PM

Subject: Re: lies

Connor, can you hear me screaming? Can you hear anything I'm saying to you? I scream and scream and nobody hears me all they hear is their own voices in their own heads telling them what they want to hear and you can't hear me even though you think you do. No one can hear me don't you see? I'm on a different frequency you're down there with everyone else and their polite society their please and thank-you their going to work and paying taxes but that's a different world than the one I live in I live up here where things don't add up the same way where one plus one does not equal two and blue and yellow do not make green and space and time have spikes and gravity shifts around one moment you're flying and the next you're a pancake on the highway and the cars are running over you one after another after another and it doesn't hurt that's the best thing none of this hurts not even precious you and your good intentions not everyone's broken love bouncing around aimlessly it's all broken Connor all of it you are broken even when you seem so solid there are tiny little cracks microscopic I cannot count on you because the cracks will just get bigger maybe not today but soon and you will break apart you will dissolve you will turn into sand if I try to hold you don't you see? I live up here and you live down there and if the worlds try to combine everything will break and there will be nothing left I will break you Connor I will break you until you're nothing. Stop trying to trick me stop saying all these nice things trying to convince me you are made of something sturdy there is nothing sturdy the air is unstable our worlds collide and explode in midair but it doesn't hurt me nothing hurts me Trevor doesn't hurt me because he is air because he knows I'm air and he doesn't need me to be anything else but you love an imaginary girl she is solid she is not me I will never be as perfect as her I will never be as perfect as you and you will love her because you will think she is solid but she will break apart until you hate her I'm sorry I'm sorry I'm sorry

Isabel,

I'm going to talk to my mom tonight when she gets home from work. Maybe you'll hate me forever. Maybe you'll never trust me again. But I'm willing to risk that. You being mad at me is a better alternative than you not existing at all. I'm going to tell my mom what's going on and we're going to find a way to get ahold of your parents. I don't know what's going to happen, but it's better than this. Maybe someday you'll forgive me. Maybe someday you'll realize that we are both solid despite the cracks.

I love you,

Connor

From: yikes!izzy

To: condorboy

Date: Friday, February 24—5:44 PM

Subject: Re: lies

You are dead to me and I am gone now I am leaving I am going somewhere you can't find me I am going somewhere I won't break

From: condorboy

To: yikes!izzy

Date: Friday, February 24—6:51 PM

Subject:

Isabel,

Can you please try to calm down for a minute? Can you just try to see things from my perspective? Try to understand how scary this must be for me. Read your emails and then try to tell me you're fine.

I talked to my mom. She wants to help, Isabel. I promise, you can trust her. She told me that a lot of mental illnesses start in the teen years. There's nothing to be ashamed about. There are a lot of medications to help and she can give you some recommendations of therapists and psychiatrists in Seattle. She also thought it'd be good for you to find out if anyone in your family has a history of mental illness, specifically bipolar disorder, because a lot of times it's genetic.

Give me your phone number. Please, Isabel. Maybe you just need to talk to someone. Maybe you just need to get out of your head.

Love,

Connor

From: condorboy

To: yikes!izzy

Date: Friday, February 24—7:36 PM

Subject:

    Isabel, if you want I can come over right now. I can get on the next ferry and be at your house in two hours.

Love,

Connor

From: condorboy

To: yikes!izzy

Date: Friday, February 24—8:11PM

Subject:

I've called everyone in the Seattle phone book with your last name. I left a voice mail for one that I'm sure was yours. Are your parents' names Dean and Linda? I told them to call me. I'm sorry, Isabel. Please don't hate me.

Love,

Connor

From: condorboy

To: yikes!izzy

Date: Saturday, February 25—3:03 PM

Subject:

Dear Isabel,

I just talked to your mom. She said you ran away. She's really scared, Isabel. She was crying. Are you happy now? You've made your point. You've forced everyone to admit how much you mean to them. Now we're all regretting all the bad things we've ever done to you. You have all the power now. Is that what you wanted?

The police said they won't look for you because you're eighteen. So I guess you're free now. How does it feel? Is it everything you ever dreamed about? Is it liberating to drive around in a car that will eventually run out of gas, with no job and nowhere to go? Your parents put a freeze on your bank card, so you can't get too far. I'm sorry if I sound a little harsh, but I guess there's some anger mixed up in all this sadness and fear. I'm angry that you're gone. I'm angry that you never let me help you. I'm angry that you waited to tell me you loved me at the same time you promised I'd never see you again.

Come back, Isabel. You're not going to get in trouble. What's going on is not your fault. You're sick and you need help. My mom knows a really great place you can go where they can help you so you don't have to feel like this anymore. Isn't that what you want? Don't you want to feel normal again?

Fuck, I don't even know if this is helping. Maybe everything I write is just pissing you off even more and pushing you further and further away. I don't know what to do. My mom keeps saying it's not my fault you ran away, but a part of me can't believe her. Maybe if I had checked my email during my trip, maybe if I had written you back sooner, maybe this wouldn't have gone so far. She says I have no control over whatever's happening inside you, whatever chemicals are misfiring in your brain, and logically I know that's true. But somehow I feel like I should have been able to reach inside you and massage you back to normal. Somehow, by sheer willpower and love, I should have been able to bring you back to reality. Mom says I need to let go and accept what's happening, but I can't give up thinking that maybe I could have helped you by just loving you enough.

It sounds ridiculous, I know. But there's always been a piece of you you've never let me see, a dark place you've never let me in, and I can't help but think there's a solution there, an answer to this riddle, some sort of truth in that unknown place where I've never had access. Maybe you were trying to protect me by never letting me see it. Maybe you were trying to keep me away from things that would convince me you weren't the perfect girl you thought I wanted you to be. But you never asked me what I wanted, Isabel. You never heard me tell you that I want everything, not just the perfect pieces, not just the sparkling, charming snapshots of you. You never let me tell you that I want every piece of you, even the broken ones, even the dark places where scary things hide.

Love,
Connor

From: condorboy

To: yikes!izzy

Date: Sunday, February 26—5:39 PM

Subject: appendages

Dear Isabel,

    I'm going to pretend you're still there, just on the other side of Puget Sound, in your bedroom surrounded by art-covered walls, looking at the computer screen and thinking of me. I'll pretend that your world is now big enough to include me, that there is room for a story besides your own, that you are no longer empty and needing to suck in everything around you. I'm trying to remember the last time you asked me anything about my life, even a simple, *How are you?* It's been a long time since I've been anything more than an appendage or a mirror. I'm starting to understand why. My mom has been telling me a lot about bipolar disorder, which is what she thinks you probably have. So I understand that certain things are symptoms and that you have no control over them, and I'm okay with that, and I don't blame you. But it feels weird for things to have gotten so one-sided, like there's this huge tilt in one direction, but now the heavy thing weighing everything down is gone and all of a sudden the balance is off and everything's bouncing around not knowing where to go. And I guess I got kind of comfortable with the focus being on you, and now that you're gone I don't know where to focus, and I feel like a huge part of me is missing. According to my mom, this is codependent behavior. I guess I got comfortable living in your shadow because it seemed like the only way to stay close to you.

Shrinks have an obsession with naming things. Bipolar, codependent, depressed, alcoholic, whatever. To her credit, Mom kept emphasizing that she can't diagnose you without meeting you, and I guess I'm kind of guilty for pushing her into giving me an explanation. So don't blame her for labeling you and putting you in a box, because I know that's what you're doing. I admit I kind of tricked her into it. All she cares about, all any of us care about, is that you come home safe and get help. It doesn't matter what anyone calls you as long as you find a way to start feeling healthy again. So please don't obsess about some stupid, arbitrary name some doctor gave to a few symptoms you seem to have. Okay, Isabel? Don't freak out on me.

Love,
Connor

From: condorboy

To: yikes!izzy

Date: Monday, February 27—8:14 PM

Subject: rain and robots

Dear Isabel,

I'm imagining that you're off in some tropical paradise right now, listening to waves lap against the sand. Maybe you've outrun the rocks and barnacles here. Maybe you've made it safely to a softer, kinder place.

It's been raining for a week. Is it raining where you are? Señor is depressed and refuses to go outside. Mom even bought her a little doggy raincoat, but as soon as it was on, her tail went between her legs and she looked as embarrassed as a dog could possibly look. We're all suffering from the winter malaise, I guess. Everything's moving a little slower than usual, as if I'm running through mud.

There was a period of time when I was little when I was convinced I was the only real human on Earth. Everyone else were robots posing as humans, even my parents. I was the only one who really felt feelings and thought thoughts, the only one who had a soul. Of course, I never stopped to ask myself why I thought this, what proof there was to support this theory. I remember it as something I just felt deep down inside, that it was just impossible that all these people around me could have their own internal worlds that were as real and important as mine.

But why would a robot need to drink a bottle of wine and stare into a fire all night? There are things going on inside my mom that have nothing to do with her being my mom. I guess part of growing up is realizing more and more that the world doesn't revolve around you.

Now I must try to convince Señor Cuddlebones to brave the drizzle for her nightly walk. She's looking at me right now with an eyebrow raised, as if saying, "I know what you're thinking, and it stinks."

Love,

Connor

From: condorboy

To: yikes!izzy

Date: Wednesday, February 29—7:55 PM

Subject: college

Dear Isabel,

Guess what! Jeremy has finally decided he wants to go to Reed! Of course he hasn't officially been accepted because it's not April yet, but it would pretty much be impossible for him to not get in. And in case you were wondering, I've known for a long time that I wanted to go to Evergreen State, but I tried not to say too much because I didn't want you to think I was following you, but now that doesn't seem like such a big deal. They accept pretty much anyone, so it looks like we'll all be neighbors next year! I'm excited for you to meet Jeremy. I know you'll really like him. In fact, you'll probably like him more than you like me. The two of you will become best friends and become Big and Important in the cool Portland scene, and you'll forget about little old me up in the forest by Olympia. It's okay. I'll have the squirrels to keep me company. And the slugs. Always the slugs.

Jeremy's already started doing all this research on the biology professors at Reed and planning what classes he's going to take for the next four years. He wants to be the world's most renowned ichthyologist. Do you know what that is? I didn't either. It's a person who studies sharks and other cartilaginous fish. What's a "cartilaginous fish?" you may ask. It's fish like sharks and rays that have cartilage instead of bone. "What's cartilage?" you may ask. It's that hard, fleshy stuff inside your ears and nose. Now don't you feel smarter? Jeremy has already informed me that during Shark Week on the Discovery Channel this summer, I am not allowed to bother him because he'll be glued to the television the whole time. Maybe something about growing up on an island has skewed his brain toward this interest in sea life. But then again, I've grown up here too and the only thing I find interesting about fish is how delicious they are when they're battered and deep-fried and slathered in Ivar's tartar sauce.

Jeremy found a dead four-feet-long six-gill shark on the beach when he was ten. Apparently this is a big deal because most sharks have five gills and not much is known about this particular species because they usually live in really deep water. So there was little ten-year-old Jeremy hauling this big-ass shark home with him, up the hill to his house and into the garage, and it weighed as much as he did, and it was all slimy and fishy from the early stages of decomposition. Then he got a big knife from the kitchen so he could dissect it, and for the next three hours, until his mom found him and freaked out and hosed him off with the garden hose, Jeremy studiously dissected that shark, carefully peeled back its skin, removed its organs, and lovingly laid them out on newspaper.

He tried to explain his excitement to me, and his eyes got all big and he was waving his hands all over the place and he kept saying, "Don't you get it? I got to *look inside*? I got to see how it *worked*." And I tried to pretend I was as excited as he was, but he could tell I had no idea what the big deal was. And it made me feel bad for a while, until a couple days later when I was trying to explain to him why I was so proud of this sculpture I was working on in art class, and he gave me what must have been the same blank look as I had given him. We laughed about that for a little while, how it's impossible to really communicate about an obsession with someone who's obsessed about something completely different. But what you can talk about is the *feeling* of obsession, so at least we have that in common. He's obsessed with knowing stuff and I'm obsessed with making stuff, and it's kind of better that way because there's no chance of us getting competitive.

Which makes me wonder: Have you ever felt competitive with me? About art and stuff? I don't think I've ever felt that way about you, mostly because I've always been too busy thinking about how brilliant you are. I guess it's hard to be competitive when you've already accepted that someone's more talented than you. It's like, why bother?

What does it feel like to be so talented? You know you are, right? It'd be impossible for you not to know it. What does it feel like to be called brilliant? I doubt I'm the first one to call you that.

Sometimes I wonder why you and Jeremy are even friends with me. I really am serious about being paranoid that the two of you are going to become best friends next year and forget all about me. You're *you* and Jeremy's *Jeremy* and you're both so fucking *special* all the time. At ten years old, Jeremy knew he was going to be a scientist, and that he was gay, and he announced both things to his parents around the same time. And ever since, he's been pushing through life with a confidence that's just not natural for a teenager. Isn't this when you're supposed to be miserable and in the throes of a constant identity crisis? It's not fair that he gets to just skip that part. But then again, if anyone deserves to be happy, it's him. And god, imagine if he was growing up anywhere else on earth. A teenage Gay Scientist in some backward town that refuses to teach evolution in school and thinks homosexuality can be prayed away? He'd be a goner. Sometimes I forget how lucky I am to live here, that outside of here, people die every day for just being themselves.

Do you ever think about that? Like, what if we were born in

some redneck town in the Bible Belt, or in Palestine, or Sudan, or Afghanistan? We complain about our lives and how no one understands us, but then I think about places like that and I just feel like an asshole.

Love,
Connor

From: condorboy

To: yikes!izzy

Date: Friday, March 2—10:50 PM

Subject: losing it

Dear Isabel,

I did my best at pretending things were normal, that I'm not terrified every second of the day, that I'm not having trouble sleeping because I'm awake worrying about you. I'm not really sure what I thought I'd accomplish by pretending you're there. Maybe some people can lie to themselves like that, but I can't. I can't not think about the fact that you're missing. I can't not think about the fact that you've been gone for five days. It seems like my mom is on the phone with your parents all the time now. She's never even met you, but it's like you're family, like your family is family. And I guess there's some comfort in that, having this connection. It's nice to know that I'm not the only one falling apart.

I talked to your sister today, and of course I immediately liked her. It's probably impossible for me to not love someone you love. When you come back, she said we should come over for dinner, you and me, like a double date with her and Karen. And something about that made me so happy, the thought of us doing something so normal and couple-y, and I was smiling like crazy, and Gennifer even said, "I can hear you smiling," and then I laughed a little, then all of a sudden I don't know what happened, but that little laugh turned into crying, and the crying turned into choking, and then I couldn't breathe. I could hear your sister asking me what was wrong, but her voice got smaller and smaller until I hung up the phone, and I was just sitting there trying to suck in air but nothing was getting in. It felt like my eyes were burning, my throat was burning, every-thing was so hot and tight like my head was going to explode. And somehow I made it downstairs, and my mom took one look at me and she got this look on her face that just made me lose it, like seeing me like that hurt her, like actually physically hurt her, and something about that just made me let go inside, like I didn't have to hold everything together anymore, like she could hold some of my pain for a while. So I let her. I went over and threw myself on the couch and let her put her arms around me and rock me like I was a little kid. And even though I was crying harder than I ever remember crying, even though I was sick with fear that I lost you, something about being held like that made it bearable. Somehow just knowing there was that space for my pain, I don't know, maybe it didn't hurt so much.

Isabel. Come home. Someone needs to hold you like that. We all need to hold you like that. You don't need to carry all your pain alone.

Love,
Connor

Dear Isabel,

My whole life, I've had this feeling like I was the one holding everything together. After my dad left when I was six, I somehow knew I was the only thing that could make my mom stop crying. I could sing a stupid song or tell her a joke or draw her a picture and she'd come back to the world, she'd come back to me. She was the one who got to be sad and lonely and stressed out, like she was the only one who got left, and I had to be the one to relieve her of those feelings. I had to be the reason she'd even *want* to be relieved of those feelings. It's a role I'm used to, and I guess that's the role I took with you, too. The solid one. The stable one. The one who's always trying to save you.

But it's hard to have your own feelings when you're always busy worrying about someone else's, when everyone's counting on you to be happy and dependable. I've always had this fear that if I ever got too confused or sad or got in too much trouble, my mom would fall apart, like somehow I was responsible for holding her together. And if she fell apart, then *everything* would fall apart. So basically, I was like this little tiny Atlas holding the world on my kid shoulders, and I'm still doing it, and the world is still heavy, and it's getting heavier and heavier every day you're gone. And I don't think I can hold on much longer. I'm afraid I'm going to let go, and the world is going to come crashing down and smash into a million pieces until all we have is rubble and we have to pick through the ruins looking for signs of life.

Love,
Connor

From: condorboy

To: yikes!izzy

Date: Sunday, March 4—10:42 PM

Subject:

I don't know what to say anymore. I don't know what I'm writing to. You're not there. These words are just turning into little lost ones and zeroes. They're not reaching you. They're not going anywhere.

You're gone. You're really gone.

From: yikes!izzy

To: condorboy

Date: Tuesday, March 6—11:29 PM

Subject: Re:

Connor,

I've come crawling back with my crooked tail between my legs, my car running on vapors, me running on vapors. Things were sharp and then they weren't. The world was shiny and bold, and now it's not. And when I try to remember what happened, I see myself on a train track, trying to outrun the train that is honking like crazy. And I should be scared, but I'm not. And everyone is yelling at me to get out of the way, but I can't hear anything real. All I hear is the poison inside my head, the voices that sound like me but are not me, the ones telling me to keep running. And I guess I'm here because the train finally caught up with me. The voices screamed as loud as they could, but it was no use. I was hit. It shut them up. And things are still, too still. It is quiet, so quiet the only thing I can hear is myself. And I can't stand it.

Connor, something is very wrong. I don't know who I am anymore. I don't know who that girl was that ran away, who did all the things I did. I think she's gone now, but what's left in her place is just garbage, all the trash she made that she didn't want to take with her. I have to deal with all the fallout. I'm the one who has to clean up her mess.

I drove to Portland and I found Trevor. That's what I did. I cannot explain why. Whatever logic I was working with has left me. I remember vague, alien thoughts that seem like they came from someone else's mind, thoughts that convinced me Trevor was the one I was supposed to be with. Because he doesn't expect anything from me, because he doesn't need me to be someone I'm not, because he treats me like the piece of shit I am. And there seemed to be some justice in that, and I remember feeling a kind of comfort in just letting go of any expectations. And for a few moments, I felt free, like everything finally made sense, like I could just finally stop trying, I could give up, and that was the key to happiness.

I have all these words and different ways to

use them, but I can't think of any way to put them together to explain how it feels to have absolutely no idea how I could have come to the conclusions I did. Is this what my brother feels like all the time, after so many years of being totally out of control? At least addicts have the excuse of some foreign chemical entering their body and skewing their judgment. But what's my excuse? Is it that I'm crazy? Is that enough to get me off the hook?

I remembered something that happened months ago, when I was hanging out with Trevor and a couple of his friends, and they were high and making fun of his apartment in Portland. The building was called Excalibur, and they seemed to think that was the funniest thing ever. I had never even been there, but I could imagine it as they described the logo written in a gaudy Old English font on the entrance, the picture of a helmet and sword on the front door. They were laughing about Excalibur and talking in these fake British accents and pretending to sword fight, and I remember thinking to myself, *These guys are supposed to be cool*. They're covered in tattoos and don't dance at concerts, but here they are stoned and climbing around on the furniture and waving imaginary swords at each other.

But that's not what I was thinking a week ago when I decided to leave. I was just thinking of Excalibur, the destination. The ridiculous word was pumping through my head like some kind of fucked-up mantra, leading me south to Portland and what I thought was my destiny. In those four hours in the car, I wrote the whole story of my life. Trevor and I would be together, I would be a devoted band girlfriend, I would go to college and do well, but it wouldn't matter because his band would make it big and we'd get married. And even if he treated me like shit, even if he cheated on me and was on tour most of the year, I wouldn't have to worry about the important stuff like food and shelter. Because that's all I really deserved anyway. I could be happy with that. It was asking too much to want anything else.

I found Excalibur. There was a parking spot right in front, and I took that as a sign that it was meant to be. I sat there for a while, practicing what I was going to say, imagining him taking me in his arms and whisking me into his apartment. And I wasn't scared. There was a sense of the inevitable, like when you're falling in dreams but it still feels like flying, before you start thinking of the inevitable crash. It was like someone else was moving me as I got out of the car and walked to the front door, as I walked into the building and found his last name on a mailbox, as I climbed the stairs and stood in front of apartment 203, as I knocked and felt nothing.

A woman answered the door. She was pretty but tired. She was holding a baby. She said, "Can I help you?" I said, "Is Trevor here?" but already I knew the answer, already I had given up. She said, "Who are you?" and I didn't say anything. She said, "I'm Trevor's wife," and I just nodded and started backing away. She said, "Who are you?" and I said, "Nobody."

Nobody. I'm nobody.

I didn't feel sad. I didn't cry. I felt emptied out, like something was pulled out from inside me, and it wasn't an uncomfortable feeling. I felt weightless. I floated across the street and toward Hawthorne. My head was empty. I wandered around, in and out of shops, for hours. I inspected the things they were selling, filling my head with every single detail, filling it so full of useless information there wasn't room for anything that could hurt me. There was a record store full of beautiful people. One of them spoke to me. I don't remember what we talked about. But I went with him when he left, I went with him when he went to the bar next door, I went with him after hours of drinks, I went with him back to his apartment.

I don't want to tell you about the next few days, not because I don't want you to know, but because I don't want to think about it. Maybe I will tell you later, after it's faded a little, when it's not so fresh, when the memories are just a hazy black and white instead of this sharp color. I don't know who I was for those days I spent in his apartment. I don't know who that girl was that was drinking those drinks and snorting those drugs. Something inside me shut off. Maybe it's a gene we all have in my family, and my brother just tapped into it more. Who knows. But I think I understand him better now. I think I understand the appeal of just throwing yourself away.

And then I woke up. It was morning and I was in bed with this guy whose last name I never knew. There was a full ashtray on the table next to my head, and the smell of it mixed with his drunk breaths. It was raining, and I felt a strong desire to run outside and just let the rain soak me, like maybe some of it could get inside and wash me out. The rain seemed to slow everything down, seemed to dull whatever convictions I had had the past week. I could remember what happened like scenes in a movie, but I no longer had a connection to what had motivated me. My evil twin was gone. She had left me in the night, left me to deal with her destruction.

She taught me how to leave. So that's what I did. I got in my car and drove the only direction I knew. My dad was home when I got here. He cried and held me until I had to push him off. I told him I was tired. He said okay. So now I'm in my room, writing to you, getting this all down in case it's gone when I wake up. Because I have a feeling everything's going to be different tomorrow. I'm going to go downstairs and life is going to be waiting for me, and I'm actually going to have to deal with it. Maybe I'm ready. Maybe I'm not. But I don't think I really have a choice.

Thank you. For being solid. For everything that you are.

Love,
Isabel

From: condorboy

To: yikes!izzy

Date: Wednesday, March 7—8:57 PM

Subject: imperfect words

Dear Isabel,

I've been sitting in front of this computer for half an hour, trying to find the perfect first sentence for this note to you. But as you can see, I didn't find it. There are too many things in the way of the words, too many conflicting feelings, and there is no way to articulate what I want you to hear. But I guess I can start by saying I love you. And yes, there may also be the fact that I'm *in love* with you, but that seems so irrelevant now. It seems like such a small, meaningless thing. That's not the kind of love you need right now. You need something bigger. Because in some ways, being in love with someone is a very selfish kind of love. It demands something of them, doesn't it? It requires some sort of reciprocation, a kind of emotional contract. You tell someone you're in love with them, and you expect something in return. And if the feeling is not matched, then you have a problem. Because you still have this expectation, this hole to be filled, and you're convinced that the other person is the only one who can fill it. But they're telling you that they can't, that they're not even going to try, but you still have this hole inside you, this place you've made to hold another person, and you can't just make it go away. So you end up hating this person you're in love with, because you need them in order to be whole, and their saying no feels like they're ripping out that piece of you. Every time you think of them, it's like they're ripping it out over and over and over.

I'm not quite sure where I meant to go with that. Basically, I wanted to say that the kind of love I want to give you right now is the kind without any of those expectations. I don't want you to feel like you owe me anything, that you need to act a certain way, that you need to pretend things are fine if they aren't. I'm just going to love you, and hopefully some of it flies off of this island and over the water and finds its way to you. Hopefully it finds somewhere cozy inside you to hang out for a while and keep you company. Hopefully you know it is there and it makes things a little more bearable.

There are more things to say, but they can wait.

Love,
Connor

From: yikes!izzy

To: condorboy

Date: Thursday, March 8–11:58 PM

Subject: Re: imperfect words

Connor,

Tell me you hate me. Tell me you're pissed at how selfish and irresponsible I've been. Tell me I'm stupid and reckless and crazy. That, I can take. That, I can wrap my hands around and hold and know it is true.

I've hurt you, Connor. I've taken advantage of your kindness and patience. I've made everything about me. I've hurt you and hurt you and hurt you, and then I come around begging to be loved again, and you just do it every time. You say you don't want to ask anything of me, but hasn't that been the problem? You always giving and giving, and me taking and taking? It's not fair. None of this is fair. I shouldn't be able to come back to everyone loving me, delusional about some kind of magic mental illness that gets me off the hook, that takes away all responsibility, like I'm some kind of victim of my brain chemistry. I think your mom has brainwashed my family, and I mean that in the nicest way possible. They have this idea in their heads that everything's going to be fine as soon as I start seeing a therapist and taking medication, that we can just forget any of this happened and everything's going to go back to normal and I'm going to be their brilliant little daughter again. But what if I don't want to take their stupid magical pills? What if I don't believe in medicine like they do? What if I don't believe in any of this?

I am responsible, Connor. I'm responsible for all of this. Maybe you all think the best thing to do is forgive me, but you're wrong. Maybe what I really need is to be punished. Maybe everyone needs to just let me go. Maybe you should just ignore me. Maybe you should hurt me as much as I hurt you.

Isabel

From: condorboy

To: yikes!izzy

Date: Friday, March 9—6:48 PM

Subject: Re: imperfect words

Fine, Isabel. You want me to tell you the other stuff? You want me to punish you? Will that make you feel better? I used to think I understood you, but now I'm not so sure any more. So even though I don't think you know what you're talking about, I'll do what you tell me. Because that's what I've always been good at, isn't it? At least lately. Maybe this summer we were something like equals, with you perhaps the more colorful one. But there was a give and take, a reciprocity that hasn't been there for a long time. Yes, you've been selfish. The world has revolved around you, your need has sucked up everything I could possibly give. You have never shown the slightest interest in my life. That is not friendship. That is not what friends do. You have been a horrible fucking friend, and a smarter person would have given up on you a long time ago.

But I am obviously not that smart. And I've started to hate myself for it, for giving everything to you so freely. The fucked-up thing is that you never forced me to do anything. It was all my choice. Don't you see? I've wanted to love you all this time; I've wanted to dote on you and heal you and lose myself. And part of me wants to blame you, wants to hate you for that, but deep down I know it's my issue, not yours. No one can really make anyone do anything unless they have a gun to their head. And maybe you could say you had a sort of emotional gun to my head. Maybe your sorrow and confusion and mania and danger scared me into submission. And maybe you have some responsibility in that. God, I don't fucking know anymore.

Do you want to know what I'm really upset about? And by upset, I mean scared, not angry. I was scared every time you refused help, every time someone who loved you said they were worried about you and you responded as if they wanted to hurt you. Even though you knew your life was unraveling, that you were unraveling, you still thought you had control. You wouldn't accept that maybe somebody knew better than you. And that stubbornness took you away from us, away from yourself. That stubbornness will kill you if you don't give it up. And I cannot accept that. I will not let that happen.

Isabel, listen to me. You will take those fucking pills and you won't whine about it. You will talk to the doctors and do what they tell you and you will get better. It may not be easy. It may be hard work. It may be the hardest and most painful thing you've ever had to go through. But whoever said life was supposed to be easy? Whoever said you were entitled to some sort of charmed life? People struggle, Isabel. That's part of life. Just because you're beautiful and brilliant and talented does not mean you're exempt from pain.

Fuck, I don't know if anything I say even gets through to you. I don't know if anything I do makes any difference at all.

Connor

From: condorboy

To: yikes!izzy

Date: Sunday, March 11—6:11 PM

Subject:

Isabel, talk to me. I know you're there.

Love,

Connor

From: yikes!izzy

To: condorboy

Date: Monday, March 12—2:13 PM

Subject: I'm sorry

Dear Connor,

   I'm sorry I haven't been taking your calls. I
pretend to be sleeping whenever I hear the house
phone ring. I don't know what I'd do if I heard
your voice. I'm afraid of it like I've never been
afraid of anything.

   Everything you said is right. Your words mix
with my parents' words and my sister's words and
spin around in my head, collect in the corner
like cobwebs. But maybe it doesn't matter anymore. Maybe I'm too fucked up to even be helped.
There was a window when I thought maybe something
was possible, a brief few hours when everything
seemed clear and I knew what to do. The morning I
woke up in that guy's bed in Portland, I just knew
I had to go home. And that gave me something to
think about for the next four hours. It gave me a
destination. And when I got home, I knew I had to
write to you. And that gave me something to think

about for a while too. Thinking of you made me feel sane. And then I went to sleep, and maybe for those hours when my eyes were closed and my body was still, maybe something inside me relaxed, and if a stranger came around and looked at me, he would think I was just a normal sleeping teenage girl. Maybe I looked like a girl who did well in school, a girl who had a boyfriend, a girl who was going to a good college. And these things would have all been true a few months ago. And maybe they could all be true now if I returned to life and got back to work. Maybe.

But those thoughts seem so translucent now, so like ghosts. When I woke up, things were black again, and they've just been getting blacker. My mom took me to a new shrink on Friday, one your mom recommended. Some little voice inside said I could trust her, but the bigger voice said what's the use? And she wrote up a prescription, and she said I'd feel better in a couple weeks, but I had to be patient. And maybe this wasn't the right drug, so maybe we'd have to try another one, and I'd have to be patient again. And maybe this would happen over and over until they found the right chemical concoction to keep me from going up and down, and she was sure that we'd get there. But I didn't want to hear "patience," I didn't want to be told maybe it wouldn't work. I know the other words were there, words like "hope," words like "getting yourself back." But those are the see-through words, the fragile things. Those are the things that break and cut you, the things you regret ever being stupid enough to believe in.

Part of me feels so done. Done with this chaos inside me, the chaos I've created in the worlds of everyone who's ever mattered to me. Done with the darkness. Done with the shame. If I was gone, none of this would matter. You'd all get your lives back. And maybe after all this taking, that's the best gift I could possibly give.

I've always doubted things. Questioned. But beneath it all, no matter how false everything seemed, I could always believe in my feelings. I always knew they were true. But now I have doctors and therapists telling me those are lies too. So now what? If everything is a lie, what do I have left?

I have you. You're the one consistent thing I can trust. But you aren't enough, Connor. I'm sorry. As wonderful and magical as you are, you can't save me. And that's not out of any weakness on your part. I know you've tried. Don't think for a second that I haven't noticed your busy little heart trying to fix all the things I break. But how could you possibly save me from myself? How could you pull out the broken pieces of me, rewire the faulty parts of my brain? Only I can do anything about that. The psychiatrist, the therapist, the doctor, my parents, my sister, you all keep saying just try, Isabel. Just be willing to try. But the truth is, I'm tired. Connor, I am so fucking tired. I don't think I can try anymore.

The therapist gave me workbooks, but even opening them seems too hard. Lying in bed and reading a couple of pamphlets about bipolar disorder seems about as hard as running a marathon. All I want to do is reread your emails. It's the only thing that really seems worth doing. It's the only thing that seems like something I can even do. That's the only world I want to live in anymore. The world of your words. The world of you loving me. But the real world is bigger than that. The real world hurts too much.

I don't want to be crazy anymore. I don't want to feel any of this. I don't want to feel anything. I could pretend I believe it's going to get better. But I would be lying. And I'm sick of lying. I'm sick of trying to protect everyone from myself. I don't think it's enough to do it for you anymore, to do it for my family. And that leaves me only one option. So now I'm saying good-bye. So now I'm the silly girl writing a suicide letter.

I'm sorry. You have to believe I'm sorry. I never meant to hurt anyone, especially you. Connor, you have loved me better than anyone.

Love always,
Isabel

I'm getting in the car. The directions to your house are taped to my dashboard. It took me this long to find you. It took me this long to decide to break your rules and do something as simple as look you up. And now maybe it's too late.

I stayed home from school today. I never stay home from school. Even when you were gone, even when no one knew where you were, I kept plugging along. But this morning my heart felt like bursting and Mom took one look at me and said I deserved a mental-health day. The irony is too horribly perfect.

So I was here to get your email. I was here to panic and call your house and your sister and your mom and my mom. And now I'm in the car and driving on this empty, tree-lined road because nobody answered. I am driving too fast because I'm trying to catch the next ferry to Seattle. I am trying to get to you before it's too late.

People do this for fun—this drive around the island, this ferry-boat ride. Tourists are up there right now, standing on the deck under the heat lamps, pointing at Seattle, pointing at the Olympics and Mount Rainier in the distance, pointing at otters and seals and jellyfish in the water. They're waving at the kayakers, waving at the fishing boats. They're smiling and taking pictures and squealing when the horn blows. They only notice how beautiful everything is.

They don't know you are somewhere dying. They don't know this big old boat is going way too slow to save you.

I am sitting in the car. I have been parked on the car deck for thirty minutes now, but I have stayed in this position, ready to go at any second. But there is nowhere to go when you're stopped and floating in the middle of the water. There is no way to make things go faster. There is absolutely nothing I can do.

We are almost there. I have been trying not to think this whole time, but sharp blasts of images keep tearing through me. Your face pale and lifeless. Bathwater stained red with blood. One thought repeats weakly, a sad attempt: Your parents don't have a gun. Your parents don't have a gun. I'm sure of it. They aren't the type. But of course that means nothing. Of course there are so many other ways to die. And you are so resourceful.

And now everyone is starting their cars. A man in a reflective vest removes a wedge from under my tire that I didn't even know was there. I jump in surprise. The car shakes and he looks at me like I'm crazy. He has no idea what's going on. None of these people know what's going on. They just think it's any old day, and they're just waiting for the cars to move so they can go shopping or whatever they do when they go to Seattle.

My phone rings. It's your mom. She got my message. I can

barely understand her because she is crying so hard. She's in her car, on her way home to you. The car in front of me pulls forward and the man in the reflective vest waves his arms at me to move. I drop the phone and it is lost somewhere under the seat, and the man is screaming at me, I can see it on his face, but the words don't make it through the window. I am trying to drive and look for the phone at the same time, and I can't hear your mom or the man in the reflective vest even though I know they're both screaming.

I find the phone but she is gone. I drive down the ramp and now there are so many men in reflective vests waving me along. And I think of you. I think of the boat ride to camp and all the stops at the other little islands on the way. I think of that island where the nuns operate the ferry terminal, where instead of these big, burly men, it's the island monastery's nuns, in habits instead of vests, wrapping the rope and speaking through walkie-talkies and waving the tourists along. You told me they prayed for us every time we departed. "Us?" I remember saying, thinking you knew something I didn't. "They pray for everyone, silly," you said. "They're nuns. That's what they do."

Everything is going too slow. The sign in the terminal says 5 mph and I want to drive right into it. I try calling your mom again but she doesn't answer. I try calling your house, and as it rings, I wonder if you can hear it. Are you there, alive, choosing *not to answer the phone? Is this all just some sick trick you're playing to see who comes running, so you can see who loves you the most?*

The streets wind around buildings full of people working. I can see the ballpark to my right, the Space Needle to my left, a steep hill in front of me. I just go the way my directions tell me, find Madison Avenue, keep driving forward, then only 3.1 miles across town until the next turn, when I will be only a few blocks from your house. As I climb the hill, I see more men holding hands. I try to picture any of them with Jeremy, but they are too old. I hope you will take good care of each other at Reed. Don't let him date anyone too lame.

But what if you never make it there? Will they just replace you with the next person on the waiting list, no big deal, like the reason you're gone is that you just chose to go to a different school?

There are too many stoplights. Too many buses. Too many people jaywalking and demanding I stop. I feel the time running out as I wait for this light to turn green. I feel my lungs deflate the longer I'm kept from you.

Drive. Just drive.

Breathe.

I am going down the hill now. There are fewer businesses and more houses. Fewer stoplights, fewer cars. Up another hill and the houses are getting bigger. The trees are getting taller. The speedometer says the car is going faster, but everything seems slowed down. The closer I get, the longer it seems to take. The directions say I'm almost there. Turn right here. The street is silent and wide and lined with almost-mansions. Two blocks. Three. One more turn and then I'm there.

And now I see the ambulance. The police car. The fire truck. The red lights spinning round and round, lighting up everything like a morbid disco ball. The neighbors standing around. A car parked in the middle of the street. Is that your mother's car? Did she leap out while it was still moving, too scared to even take the time to park? Why is there a fire truck?

I pull into someone's driveway. I get out. I run. The door to your house is open. I step inside and it seems like a movie set. You cannot really live here. I hear voices upstairs. I run. I am scared but I run. I close my eyes and I run.

There are firemen in the hallway. They are big and in my way, but I am fast and I get through them. There is a woman who must be your mother. She is leaning against the wall. She has her hands in front of her eyes. The men in uniform are all looking through the doorway, your doorway. They are all looking at you. All these men who do not know you, and it is your mother who has her eyes closed.

On the floor. You. With your eyes closed. The paramedics

roll you on your side. Your arm hangs lifeless. You are wearing
pajama pants and a tank top, like you could be just any girl. The
men are on their knees around you, moving things—their bags,
their equipment. They are getting ready to do something. They
are fast. How many times have they done this before? There
is so much movement and you are too still. They are touching
your things, pushing them aside. A pair of fuzzy slippers flies
into the corner and I want to hurt the man who threw them.

He has his hand in your mouth now. I cannot watch. I scour
the walls with my eyes, searching the paintings and collages
for some kind of clue. Every inch is covered by something you
made beautiful. There are magazine models piled on top of
each other, their faces framed by torn, burnt edges. Their eyes
have been gouged out and replaced with black. Red Xs are over
their mouths. A chorus of voices silenced. What were they trying to say, Isabel? What were they screaming that made you
have to shut them up?

Someone says, "One, two, three." I look just in time to see
them shove the tube up your nose and down your throat.

And just like that, you are alive. You are coughing. You
are gagging on the tube. This is the first time I've heard your
voice in months, and it sounds like this. You are vomiting.
There is the sound of suction. Someone says, "Roll her over."
Someone says, "Make sure she doesn't aspirate." I feel your

mother behind me. "What does that mean? What does aspirate mean?" She squeezes my shoulders. I try to tell her I don't know, but nothing comes out. My throat is raw, like I'm choking on the tube too. I am holding your mother's hand. We are watching you. We are willing you not to die.

They are pumping something into you. They are pumping something out. Your eyes are still closed but I can see tears running down your cheek. "Is she going to be okay?" your mother asks, but no one answers, no one even acknowledges her question. They are setting up the gurney. They are pushing us out, like we don't even matter, like you are theirs now because they saved your life.

They saved your life, didn't they? Isn't that what just happened? The tube down your throat, the clean stuff in, the dirty stuff out. You're clean now, right?

Isabel, wake up.

The men are yelling, "Move, move, move!" We do what we're told. We run down the hall, down the stairs. We don't want to be trampled. We don't want to be the ones who keep you from getting to the hospital in time.

The neighbors stare at our strange parade. Me in the front, then your mother, then all the men in uniform, and then your body, laid out and on wheels. We stand to the side while they load you into the back of the ambulance, beautiful sleeping cargo. Your mother grasps her heart and starts weeping. One of the ambulance men tells her to drive to the hospital. She nods and says, "My keys. Where are my keys." I put my hand on her shoulder and tell her we'll find them.

I look at you. At your thin arms strapped in. Your feet bare and too vulnerable. I start to panic. You will freeze. They must do something or you will freeze. "Someone get her a blanket!" I yell. "It's freezing out here. She'll freeze to death." And as soon as that word comes out of my mouth, everything is silent and still and breaking.

"We'll take good care of her," the ambulance man says, and I have no choice but to believe him. And as he's reaching for the doors, I see the tiniest movement. Your fingers, your hand, it is moving. Your eyes are opening. You look right at me, and something inside you smiles, and just as the doors are closing, I see the side of your mouth bend, I see your lips part and form the word "Hi."

From: condorboy

To: yikes!izzy

Date: Wednesday, March 14—5:11 PM

Subject: empty

Dear Isabel,

I'm writing because it's the only thing I know how to do. My fingers type with the blind faith that you are there, even though I know you're not. And maybe these words have become something more than emails; maybe they are a kind of journal. Writing to you is like writing to another piece of myself.

You are in the hospital. You're lying in a foreign bed somewhere, your insides scraped raw from the charcoal the doctors made you drink to clean you out. The bottle of pills that was supposed to make you better became your weapon. The medicine became poison.

I came to the hospital but they wouldn't let me see you. I'm not family and you were still too fragile. I would have waited forever, but your mother sent me home, said there's not much I can do for you just sitting there. So I left, but not until after she held onto me until I couldn't breathe. I could feel her shudder as she wept. She said "thank you" in a voice so low it almost didn't sound human. Maybe mothers are the only people capable of making that sound. Our first meeting, and already we know each other too well.

So I'm at home, trying not to obsess, trying to let my mom think she's comforting me. Your mother has been calling regularly to give updates. I am trying to watch TV, but all I can see is a hospital drama starring you and your family. Your mother in constant vigil by your side. Your dad pacing the hall, beating himself up for finally going back to work and leaving you home alone that day. Your sister and Karen holding each other tight, praying to not lose their child's only aunt.

Mom says tomorrow you're going to the psych ward. You will be stabilized by then, filled up with fluids, caught up on sleep, your physical body in some sort of state resembling normal. But what about the rest of you? Are you going to be so heavily medicated you become someone else? Are they going to turn you into a zombie to save you? I don't want to picture you with blank eyes and a drooling mouth, imprisoned in some chlorine-smelling, fluorescent-lit dungeon. Mom says she's familiar with where you're staying, she knows some of the staff, and she's confident they're taking good care of you. When I picture you, it's with your hair wild, laughing, a deep red sunset and evergreens behind you. The memory smells like pine needles and salt water. Not like a hospital. Not like disinfectant and sick people. But I'll take what I can get. It's better you're there than nowhere at all.

It seems like I should be feeling differently than I do. When someone you love tries to kill themselves, there must be some protocol of grieving and fear. Maybe I'm in shock. Maybe I've used up all my pain already as I've read and reread the emails that tell the story of your unraveling. Maybe this is something I was expecting deep down, something I had unconsciously prepared for. Is it wrong for me to feel relieved? Am I a monster for feeling grateful that they finally caught you, that you're trapped and being watched so you can't hurt yourself anymore? What else could have been done?

Maybe freedom and safety will always be at war with each other, and maybe one day freedom will win. Maybe someday you can have it back, maybe someday soon, but right now it seems irrelevant. Freedom is the least of your concerns. I'm glad you're there, Isabel. I'm glad you're getting a break from holding the world on your shoulders, even if it probably feels like prison.

After all this time trying to save you, maybe I finally have. Maybe I'm the reason you're in there instead of a casket. I wonder if I'm supposed to feel proud of that. Should I pat myself on the back for calling your mom after reading your last email? Is it because of me that she called 911 and rushed home from work? What if she had picked up my message ten minutes later? An hour? What if those pills had more time to do their damage? I try not to think of these things, but I can't help it. What if I hadn't called at all? Maybe you hate me for it now, but I'm counting on you being glad someday. You'll feel better and all of this will seem like a sad mistake, and you'll look into my eyes and tell me how grateful you are to have had another chance.

Love,
Connor

Day 1

I blink and there's a blank room with two beds, two dressers, two scared strangers. If you squint your eyes just right, this could look like my first dorm room. Does college smell this much like sorrow? Can you hear so much crying through the walls?

All I can do is listen. They say I can't talk for a few days because my throat is so raw. I cough up little specs of blood. They give me lozenges that taste like sadness. God has finally found a way to shut me up.

This is not real life. This is frost.

We're not allowed to wear shoes. Regular clothes are fine, but something about shoes must threaten our sanity. They give us these little brown ankle socks, one size fits all, with the little white rubber pads on the bottom to keep us from slipping. What kind of trouble could you get in with shoes? Maybe you could hang yourself with the shoelaces. Or maybe you could run faster. Maybe you could stand just a little more sturdy.

Every two hours, I open my mouth, I lift my arm up. The thermometer tells them I'm still human. My blood pressure says my heart's still beating, or whatever blood pressure is supposed to tell. In two hours, maybe not, and then they'll have to check again. My vital signs like clockwork.

I'm becoming a chemical concoction. The doctor says I may be on Lithium for the rest of my life. Plus there's Zoloft for the depression. Ativan so I can sleep. Something else whose name I forget.

Apple juice in little cartons. Jell-O in single-serving cups.

I can project myself into these hallways. I can make myself a hologram. I walk around, in and out of rooms and chairs. I do what they tell me, no more, no less, and nobody knows that I'm not really here. The real me is somewhere else, safe for the time being in some shoe box or suitcase, an inconspicuous home for a soul.

Dear Isabel,

I talked to your sister today. She said you're doing really well. She seems like a no-nonsense kind of person, so I'm pretty sure she's telling the truth. She said everyone at the hospital is really nice and knows what they're doing, and you seem to genuinely want to do what they tell you. We laughed about that a little— you doing what you're told. It must really be serious if you're not fighting everyone every chance you get. We were sort of laughing like it was a joke, but we both knew it wasn't a joke at all. We talked about how we want to feel relieved that you're getting help, but it's a tentative kind of hope. I guess the stronger you get, the stronger the hope will get too.

It's torture not being able to see you, but I guess I understand why it should only be family at the beginning. Mom and Jeremy have been great, and it's been nice getting to know your family. But I feel like everyone's just paper cutouts of themselves, that the only real people are you and me. Señor Cuddlebones knows something's wrong and has been by my side nonstop. Sometimes I have to stop what I'm doing so I can remind myself to breathe, and it's like it's her cue to lean over and lick my hand until everything feels a little more normal. It's like a gift she has or something. My mom's friend Liza brings animals to retirement homes to cheer up the patients. I should tell her Señor Cuddlebones wants to apply for the position.

I'm talking nonsense now. I guess I don't really have a whole lot to say. It's like someone pushed a big pause button, and time is stopped. We're all just waiting for something to happen, like the president is going to make a big State of Isabel's Mental Health speech, and then we'll know what we're supposed to do with ourselves.

Love,
Connor

Day 2

It's weird writing with a pen instead of a
keyboard. It's making me have to slow down.
I'm thinking in chunks. Just like in dreams,
my wrist doesn't want to bother with transitions.
I bet in ten years kids won't even learn
how to write. Instead of practicing their
letters, they'll start doing keyboard drills in
kindergarten. And writing stuff by hand will be
this old-fashioned thing that only a few people
know how to do anymore, like sword fighting and
speaking Latin. And then when technology fails
and all the computers explode or whatever,
no one will know how to communicate and we'll
lose our written language and be like cavemen
again drawing pictures instead of words. And
maybe that's when the artists will take over,
when what we do will be important, when
everything has to be said with symbols.

It's impossible to tell how crazy everyone
is in here. This one guy looks fine, dressed up
like someone's dad you'd see mowing his lawn on
a Sunday afternoon, khakis and a sweatshirt,

psych-ward casual. But then you realize that you've never heard him speak. Then you see the forest of scars up and down his forearm. Then you're walking down the hall and hear a whisper of pain, like a movie with the volume turned low, and it gets a little louder as you walk, and then you're standing next to the Room, and you look inside the little window and there he is thrashing around, throwing himself against the padded walls, screaming at the top of his lungs. But you can only hear the muted version; you can only see him on this tiny screen.

From: condorboy

To: yikes!izzy

Date: Saturday, March 17—11:28 AM

Subject: garbage

Dear Isabel,

Jeremy went into Seattle by himself two weekends ago to hang out at some Queer Youth Center and didn't even tell me until today. I asked him why he didn't ask me if I wanted to come, and he was like, "Because of everything going on with Isabel, I didn't think you'd be interested," but I could tell that wasn't the full truth. So I kept bugging him until he admitted the real reason. He said, "Why would I ask you to come with me to hang out at the Queer Youth Center?" and I was like, "Because I'm your best friend, that's why." Then he just shook his head like I was some dumb kid and said, "I didn't really go there to find *friends*, Connor." What a bastard.

Two idiots decided to have an eating contest at lunch yesterday, so they stuffed their faces with sloppy joes until one of them barfed all over the cafeteria floor. That was the highlight of my day.

Love,

Connor

Day 3

There's a pay phone in the hall by the nurse's
office that accepts incoming calls. There's a
lady named Jane who sits by the phone all day,
like she's the psych ward secretary. She says
she's waiting for a call, but she won't say from
whom. Her face lights up when the phone rings,
but it falls just as fast as she listens to the
person on the other line ask for someone else.
She won't say anything, won't yell out who the call
is for. She'll just drop the receiver, let it hang
there on its curly cord with the person on the
line saying, "Hello? Hello?" She'll wander off, so
you have to just hope that someone else is there
to direct the abandoned calls. When you're done
talking, Jane materializes out of nowhere so she
can take back her perch and wait by the phone
again. The call is never for her.

The usual crew is wailing for pain meds
again. Yesterday, they seemed to all have
sprained ankles. Today it is migraines. Half
of the people in here are drug addicts or
alcoholics, in addition to being crazy. I try

to picture my brother here, but I can't remember what he looks like.

I can't stop puking and my hands are shaking like the alcoholic schizophrenic's down the hall. The doctor says it's probably the medication, but he made me take a pregnancy test just in case. What kind of horrible god would even think of putting a life inside me? Who's crazy now?

Top Ten Lamest Things About the Psych Ward:

10. The food
9. The way people get discharged and just leave without saying good-bye
8. Family visits
7. The lack of decorations
6. No reading after lights-out at 10:00 every night
5. The people who can't even remember how many times they've been here
4. The brown socks
3. The padded room
2. The loneliness
1. The absence of you

From: condorboy

To: yikes!izzy

Date: Sunday, March 18—3:47 PM

Subject: thawing

Dear Isabel,

It's starting to warm up finally. We've had three nights in a row with no frost, and my mom swore she saw some tulips sprouting on the way to work. I wonder if they let you outside where you are. Do they make you wear those paper hospital gowns? Well, it's definitely not warm enough outside for that kind of attire.

Your sister says all you've been doing is apologizing for freaking everybody out. Mom says that's a good sign, that you're seeing how your behavior has affected others. Gennifer says you've been promising to never do anything like that ever again, and I can hear her hope getting a little stronger. I wish I could see this new proof too. All I have is the image of you on your bedroom floor with a tube up your nose. You on the stretcher. This is all I can see, even when I try not to, and it scares me.

Love,

Connor

Day 4

There are gradations of crazy. There are types, classifications, just like anything else. There are a couple first-timers here like me. We try not to take up too much space, try to prove with our silence that we don't belong here. There are some who have been to treatment for addiction, alcoholism, and eating disorders, and they unanimously see this as a step down the recovery institution ladder. The rest seem strangely comfortable. They have visited here or somewhere like here before. Two or three came in properly crazy, talking to themselves and smelling of urine. But now they're cleaned up and look just like the smiling housewife who says she just needs to "reset her medications." There are a lot of those. People who were doing fine and leading normal lives, and then they got caught up in the illusion, started believing they were indeed as normal as they looked. Janice the swimming instructor stopped taking her meds and decided to go diving while wearing a winter coat full of bricks. Steve the publicist quit drinking, got some bad advice from an AA fundamentalist who said his psych meds were drugs and needed quitting too, then Steve ended up painting his windows black and telling his wife she had to abort their baby because it was not human.

But nobody says the word "suicide." Even the girl with bandages on her wrists doesn't mention anything about trying to kill herself. They say things like they're in here getting "recalibrated" or "reset," like they're just some malfunctioning machine that needs a reboot. Maybe it's that simple. Someone just needs to unplug me, let me cool down for a little bit, then plug me back in, good as new. Maybe I never really wanted to die. Maybe I just needed to power off. Maybe we're just robots who are only ever off or on, but we're not the ones who are supposed to decide when to flip the switch.

How do I apologize to my family for trying to kill myself? How do I sit with them on my psych ward bed and convince them I won't do it again? Every soft sound they make, every slow, deliberate movement makes me want to slap myself in the face over and over, because I can tell how hard they're trying not to startle me, like I'm some fragile, erratic thing they can't trust. And there are so many feelings I could be feeling, but the only one that makes any sense is embarrassment, and there is nothing glamorous about that. I am not the sexy genius whose brain is too big for this world. I am not the brilliant artist who speaks to angels. I am just a girl with a chemical imbalance and a family who's a little scared of me, and I can't look them in the eyes, I can't say anything better than I'm sorry. All I can do is let my sister hold my hand like she's been doing my whole life, and as she squeezes my fingers it is only those small bones that break, and nothing else feels anything close to what alive is supposed to feel like.

From: condorboy

To: yikes!izzy

Date: Monday, March 19—6:17 PM

Subject: whales

Dear Isabel,

There's been a bunch of Orca whale sightings around the island the last couple of days. Jeremy says they usually don't come this far down the Sound, so it's probably because of global warming, and they're going to get stuck in the mud flats in Olympia and die. But Mom says they've come to cheer me up. I like her explanation better.

Love,

Connor

Day 5

The good news is I'm not pregnant. The bad news is I'm still here.

There's a short nurse named Mandy, and she's my favorite. She calls me "sweetie," and when she asks me how I'm feeling it's like she actually wants to know. I thought maybe I was her favorite, maybe I was her pet or something because of all the attention she was giving me, but then I noticed her name next to mine on the white board by the nurse's office, so I guess it's just her job to pay special attention to me.

She wraps the blood-pressure belt around my arm, squeezes the ball until it holds on tight. Then it deflates and she looks like she's concentrating, and she could either be counting my heartbeats under her breath or whispering a magical incantation. I've never known how these things work, what the numbers mean, "something over something," then a nod, like I'm expected to know how to speak medicine.

She asks me if I have a boyfriend. I tell

her no, but I'm thinking of you. I try the words out in my head. "Connor. Boyfriend." And then I look around at the white walls, see Jerry the psychotic shuffling around in his pajamas, watch Mandy write something down on my charts, my life reduced to doctors' scribbles in a file, and I say the words under my breath, my own incantation. "Connor. Boyfriend." And then my heart splits open and I'm tearing at the blood-pressure thing, I'm ripping apart the Velcro, my hospital socks go flying, I want everything off, everything they've put on me. And I'm tugging at the bracelet, the plastic paper that doesn't break, the thing with the secret code that brands me as belonging to them. But it won't come off, and I start running and the floor is cold without the socks, and they catch me, of course they catch me, I don't even get halfway down the hall, and Jerry's just standing there looking at me like I'm crazy.

This is normal behavior in here. All that happens is the doctor asks me how I'm feeling. He's always asking me how I'm feeling. I keep telling him I feel better, but I don't think he believes me. It's like I'm giving him the wrong answer, like he wants me to tell him I'm falling apart, I'm hearing voices, I think I have wings and plan to fly out of here at four-thirty. No one believes me that I don't want to die. They can't believe it could be that simple, that it was all just a big mistake, that someone can want to die for a few days, make a half-assed attempt, then change their mind. Or maybe I'm just lying to myself that it's that easy. Maybe I'm forgetting. Maybe I'm not as well as I think I am. Is it even possible for me to know?

The doctor wonders why I don't talk in group, so I tell him. It's not because I'm depressed. It's not because I'm manic. It's not because I'm up or down—it's because I'm no place at all. Medicine has erased all that, and now I'm left with this fuzzy mildew in its place. I don't want to die and I don't want to run around in circles, but I also can't think straight and I'm exhausted all the time. Is this a fair trade? Am I okay with the fact that my thoughts and feelings seem so far away and out of focus?

The doctor says it sounds like the medication is working. I ask him if this is how I'm supposed to feel. He says, "Let us try a lower dosage." I want to tell him there is no "us" here. There is just me and my hijacked brain and the wreckage I've left behind. There is just me trapped in this place with no art and no you, while he gets to leave every night to go home to his family and wake up sane.

From: condorboy

To: yikes!izzy

Date: Tuesday, March 20—10:30 PM

Subject: surprise!

Dear Isabel,

Guess what . . .

I'M COMING TO VISIT ON THURSDAY!

I'M COMING TO VISIT ON THURSDAY!

I'M COMING TO VISIT ON THURSDAY!

Can you see anything out of your window? Sometimes I look out at Seattle and pretend one of the buildings is where you are. I pick a random window and stare at it and pretend I'm looking into your eyes.

Also . . .

I'M COMING TO VISIT ON THURSDAY!

Love,

Connor

Day 6

Some people in here don't think I should go to college next year. At least not Reed. This nervous, frog-eyed woman named Jill says it's too much stress, I should stay home, maybe take a couple classes at the community college if I feel up to it, get ten hours of sleep every night, and wear a gas mask when I go outside. Jill's a hypochondriac and is scared of everything, including water, so I'm not taking advice from her anytime soon.

But I do wonder about it. What if I'm at school and I go manic and think I can fly and jump off the roof, or what if I get depressed and lock myself in my room and nobody notices until they can smell the stench of my decaying body? I feel fine now, but they're always warning us about getting too confident, "hubris," as Jeff the bipolar history professor likes to call it. It's like they're trying to make us scared of everything. They say people with bipolar disorder need to be vigilant about keeping track of their moods. Every day I'm supposed to record how I feel in a journal, even several times a day, then report my findings to my outpatient doctor. But it seems like anything could be considered a sign of impending doom; anything can trigger an episode—stress, too much caffeine, not enough sleep, lack of a consistent schedule, arguments with loved ones, loss of a pet, a loud noise, too many donuts, clowns, roller-skating. Maybe not the last few, but you see what I mean. If I start feeling irritable or horny or craving chocolate, I must sound the alert. If I lose my appetite, I should call 911. If I have a headache, I need to check myself in to the hospital. While everyone else is going to be busy worrying about their grades or if some boy likes them, I'm going to be obsessing about every little mood so I don't lose my mind.

I'm not sure what I'm doing in this journal, in these notes to you. I'm not sure what you want to hear, or what I want to be telling you. Maybe I'm supposed to be reflecting about my life, figuring out what went wrong, dissecting everything very rationally and coming up with

theories and plans and all that logical stuff.
Or maybe I'm supposed to just feel my way
to sanity, open up and talk about my childhood
and my mother and my brother and my fears
until they lose all their juice. Maybe all I
need is a good old-fashioned cry, and I can
catch my tears with this paper and mail it
to you. I could do all the exercises in this
Cognitive Behavioral Therapy workbook. I could
turn them in to you like homework. And the gold
stars will pile up—the new tools, the coping
mechanisms, the rules to live by. I could lay
everything out, draw you an annotated map of
my psyche. I could narrate my road to sanity
like a nature documentary, English accent and
all, very authoritative.

But no. You must be tired of the Isabel
Show by now. And this dramatic plot twist, so
contrived. Now is what happens behind the
scenes, the real work, the construction and
bookkeeping and all that boring stuff. I will do
what they tell me. I will take my medications
as prescribed. I will go to outpatient therapy
three days a week. And then they'll give me

back to the world one piece at a time. I'll earn my way back in. Little by little, I'll start to convince people I'm sturdy. And it won't be a show, it'll just be me, and that will have to be enough.

I wonder what it'll take for you to believe me. What do I have to do to convince you I'm solid, that you don't have to tiptoe around me with a net, waiting to catch the falling pieces? Connor, you can stop holding your breath now. You can stop losing yourself to keep me standing.

I saw you that day in the ambulance. Maybe you assumed I was out of my mind and wouldn't remember, but I do. I saw the exact same face I remember from the summer. Even through your fear, I saw everything I always loved, and for that second I felt like I was in the world again.

I try not to wonder what you saw. Certainly not the girl you remember. I think about all the almost-plans we made in the last few months, how close we came to meeting again. But I would always sabotage things, wouldn't I? It was always me canceling our plans.

I realize now I was doing it on purpose. I think I was scared of disappointing you. I was scared of you realizing I'm not who you want me to be. Part of me thought you'd keep loving me only if I could keep you at a distance. Your memories of me are part trees and part ocean and part magic, and I don't know if I will ever be that girl again. She was the best version of me. Connor, I'm so afraid of you being disappointed. I'm someone else now, someone I'm afraid you won't be able to love.

Mom says you're coming to visit on Thursday. I'm terrified. I don't want you to see me in here, in this context. For a second I thought of asking her to tell you not to come. The doctor says I can probably go home on Tuesday or Wednesday, so it wouldn't be too much to wait until I get out in a few days. I built up a whole list of excuses and explanations in my head. But it felt wrong. It's the kind of thing I've been doing my whole life—making excuses, running away from things—but somehow now it feels wrong. So I asked myself what I'm so afraid of. Am I scared of you seeing me in here? Am I scared of you knowing exactly who I am? God, I'm so tired of running and hiding from everything.

Then I remembered that there's nothing I want more than to see you right now, and I'm not going to let fear take that away from me.

From: condorboy

To: yikes!izzy

Date: Wednesday, March 21—8:25 PM

Subject: beautiful

Dear Isabel,

The sunset tonight was the red-orange of jellyfish poison, the clouds like tentacles hanging down and stinging the sea.

I don't think I'm going to be able to sleep tonight.

Love,

Connor

Day 7

I keep trying to understand why I did what I did. I try to look back on the moments, the days, the weeks before I took the pills. I try to remember what was going through my head. The weird thing is, I don't know that I was even really thinking about death. I wasn't thinking about forever or funerals or being gone for good. I wasn't thinking about anything in a long-term or permanent way. The only thing that existed was what I was feeling in those short moments. All I can remember thinking was that I wanted a way out. In that moment when I picked up the bottle of pills, I needed relief more than I ever needed anything in my life. I hurt so badly that I was willing to do anything to stop it, and nothing I could think of seemed like it would work. Not drugs, not sex, not running away, not anything. The pain was inside me, and it felt like it was never going to leave, so the only way to kill it was to kill me too.

And it all seems so temporary when I look back on it. That's something they say a lot in here: "Suicide is a permanent solution to a temporary problem." Most people roll their eyes at the saying, but it scares me every time I hear it.

And now it's only a week later, only a handful of days since I was so convinced that I wanted to die, and already I can't imagine ever feeling that hopeless. I guess a big part of it is the medication starting to work. And maybe part of it is that it's also just easier to feel better in a place like this. As crazy as it is, at least it's a break from the outside and full of people who want to help me. The only thing I really have to think about is getting better. Maybe everything will change when I go back home, back to school, back to my same old life. But I don't think so. At least I hope not. And that's really the important thing, isn't it? Hope.

God, this place has turned me into a cheeseball. Oh well.

I think of all the people who weren't as lucky as me—the people whose suicide attempts were successful. They could be alive now and feeling better. They could be trying to work through the things that cause them pain. They could find people to help them. All the people who need medication, who need therapy, the people haunted by horrible memories, the kids getting bullied, the ones who feel so alone—there are solutions for all of them. But I know that sometimes it seems easier to give up than to risk hoping that things can change. Sometimes a person can be so consumed with pain that they can't see solutions anywhere. But the solutions are there. I know they are. Help and hope are everywhere. I just hope people find them. I hope they at least try looking before they decide to give up.

Connor, I have so much to say to you. So many sorrys. But maybe before those, there is just thank you. Thank you for loving me. Thank you for saving my life.

I'm looking out the window and the sunset is something gorgeous. There are about a billion different shades of orange, more than I thought possible. I think I can see the cherry blossoms starting to bloom, and do you know how happy that makes me? There's a street by my house that's lined with cherry blossom trees, and every spring when they're in full bloom, the petals float around and fall to the ground and it's like a warm, pink snowstorm.

I can see your island, Connor. I can see Bainbridge. Maybe you're looking at the same sunset right now. Maybe you're looking at this hospital, looking at me, and don't even know it.

You're supposed to be here in eleven minutes. Eleven excruciating minutes. I don't know if I'm going to survive that long.

I can't stop looking at the clock on the wall. I considered running. I could make a break for the door when one of the nurses punches in the code. This keeps striking me as a reasonable option, but then I visualize it in fast-motion slapstick, with some kind of ridiculous circus music playing, and all the patients are all lined up in the background doing choreographed kicks. Yes, this is where my mind goes, even when I'm medicated.

What am I going to do for eleven whole minutes? What's the best way to appear not crazy? Probably not chewing your nails while sitting on a bed in a psych ward.

"Isabel, honey." It is Mandy's voice. I look over to the door. "You have a visitor."

And here you are. Eleven minutes early.

I thought I would hear you coming. I thought I'd at least have a chance to stand up and put on a smile and try to glamour us out of these surroundings. But you snuck up on me. I don't know how you did it, but you caught me unguarded, and I try to imagine your first impression, I try to remember what I was doing the moment before now, and I'm pretty sure I wasn't picking my nose or talking to myself or anything too embarrassing, but I have no idea what my face looks like when nobody's looking.

And now here you are, standing in the doorway with a

bouquet of bright flowers, and you have a smile on your face that makes me think I know exactly what you looked like as a little boy. And I'm trying not to cry, I really am, I'm holding my breath and trying to keep my smile, but the flowers you're holding are the brightest things I've seen in days, and I think I see a mustard stain on your shirt, the yellow smudge like a sunshine above the forest scene of your ironic "Washington Wonderland" T-shirt. And of all things, that's what makes me lose it. The mustard stain on your silly shirt. That's what flips the switch and starts the tears flowing, that's what opens me up, and something inside me lets go. I don't know what it is but it feels like flying, and somehow I make it into your arms and feel you warm and solid. You are real, you are actually real. All this time, I'm not sure I really believed it, but here you are in my arms, here you are in my room in the psych ward, and you are not running away.

I make the rain for your silly T-shirt, I water the trees in your Washington Wonderland. I hold your head in my hands and try to memorize the shape with my fingers, I put my face in your neck and take in the smell of you. I breathe in and let you fill me with calm. I breathe out and look you in the eye.

"Hi," you say.

"Hi," I say.

"Nice place," you say with a grin.

"Mustard," I say, pointing out the stain for you.

"I was saving it for later," you say. "Hungry?"

"Not so much."

We're standing in the doorway with our arms around each other. Mandy has disappeared. I'm looking at you and I start to giggle.

"What's so funny?" you say, and you are laughing too.

"How's this for a first date?"

"Perfect," you say.

"Very romantic," I agree.

"I brought flowers."

"Such a gentleman."

We separate, and I feel suddenly shy. I think I see you blushing. You hold out the flowers and I take them—vibrant oranges and reds and yellows, exotic flowers I don't know the names of, all of them unique and beautiful and a little bit wild.

"No carnations?" I joke.

"I asked the guy to do all carnations," you say. "But unfortunately they were out. Seems everyone else in the world already got carnations."

"Damn," I say.

"Yeah, damn," you say. You smile. "I guess we'll have to do something a little different."

ACKNOWLEDGMENTS

I would like to express my gratitude to the book *Living with Someone Who's Living with Bipolar Disorder* by Chelsea Lowe and Bruce M. Cohen, MD, PhD (Jossey-Bass, 2010). This book was invaluable to my understanding of what it's like to love someone with bipolar disorder.

As always, thanks to my agent, Amy Tipton, and editor, Anica Mrose Rissi, for your smarts, sass, and support. Thanks also to everyone at Simon Pulse for believing in my little books and working so hard for them.

Thanks to my pal Rachel B.—for having quite possibly the best smile in the whole world, and for your wisdom and generosity.

Thanks to Nana Twumasi, my friend and Virgo twin—for your superior editorial instincts and attention to detail. You continue to prove that Virgos really are better than everyone else.

Thanks to all my friends and family who have loved and embraced my crazy for all these years. You know who you are.

And biggest thanks to my husband, Brian—for asking all the right questions, and for having faith in me to find the answers.